THINK TWICE

A DCI SEAN BRACKEN NOVEL

JOHN CARSON

DCI SEAN BRACKEN SERIES
Starvation Lake
Think Twice

DCI HARRY MCNEIL SERIES
Return to Evil
Sticks and Stones
Back to Life
Dead Before You Die
Hour of Need
Blood and Tears
Devil to Pay
Point of no Return
Rush to Judgement
Against the Clock

Where Stars Will Shine – a charity anthology compiled by Emma Mitchell, featuring a Harry McNeil short story –
The Art of War and Peace

DI FRANK MILLER SERIES
Crash Point
Silent Marker
Rain Town
Watch Me Bleed
Broken Wheels
Sudden Death
Under the Knife
Trial and Error
Warning Sign
Cut Throat
Blood from a Stone
Time of Death

Frank Miller Crime Series – Books 1-3 – Box set
Frank Miller Crime Series - Books 4-6 - Box set

MAX DOYLE SERIES
Final Steps
Code Red
The October Project

SCOTT MARSHALL SERIES

Old Habits

THINK TWICE

Copyright © 2021 John Carson

Edited by Charlie Wilson at Landmark Editorial
Cover by Damonza

John Carson has asserted his right under the Copyright, Designs and Patents Act 1988, to be identified as the author of this work.

This is a work of fiction. Names, characters, places, brands, media, and incidents are either the products of the author's imagination or are used fictitiously. Any resemblance to actual events, locales, or persons, living or dead, is coincidental.

Without limiting the rights under copyright reserved above, no part of this publication may be reproduced, stored in or introduced into a retrieval system, or transmitted, in any form, or by any means (electronic, mechanical, photocopying, recording, or otherwise) without the prior written permission of the author of this book. Innocence is and

All rights reserved

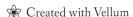 Created with Vellum

To R.L.

ONE

'I've killed twenty-seven people so far this year. One of you is next.'

He looked around the room at the expectant faces. All eyes were on him now, watching his expression, his every movement. Nobody said a word, but their eyes didn't leave his face.

His hand reached into the bag and they were mesmerised. He rummaged around and pulled his hand back out quickly, like a snake had bitten him.

Some in the small crowd gasped, some smiled, others laughed.

Edwin Hawk held the piece of paper high and smiled at the room, looking at the group.

'And that name is...' He unfolded the piece of paper and read the name. 'Maxine Campbell!'

There were squeals of delight from a woman, who

smiled at the man sitting beside her.

'Congratulations, Maxine!' Hawk said. 'You will be in my next book as one of the victims. But wait – if you want to be, you can be a good guy!'

'Oh no, I want to be a bad guy!' Maxine said, her voice shrill with excitement.

'Your wish is my command.' He looked around at everybody. 'Thank you all for taking part in the bidding. I greatly appreciate you all.'

A woman sidled up to him. 'It's us who appreciate you, Dr Hawk.' She smiled at him.

'Please, just call me Hawk. Everybody does.'

The woman's cheeks were rosy, either from excitement or rushing about behind the scenes. 'Hawk it is.' She turned to the room. 'I'm sure that we can all stay for refreshments?'

The small gathering assured her that they could. People stood up from their chairs and started to move towards the buffet at the back of the room.

'Thank you so much for allowing us this little get together tonight.' The woman, Helen Moore, was acting like she was about to be deflowered at her high school dance and was hoping the experience would be exactly as she had imagined it.

'Helen, it's always a pleasure to see you when I come to Edinburgh. This Writers' Museum is older than the city where I live.'

'You're so kind, Hawk. I know you've been on a busy tour, and for you to find the time to come and see us is extremely kind.'

'I can't think of a better way to spend my time. I'm staying in Edinburgh to bring in the bells, as you Scots say it.'

'Maxine is one of the trustees for the Writers' Museum events, and I know she'll be delighted to have her name used in your book.' Helen wrung her hands together for a moment. 'Maybe just not as a prostitute. Maxine lives in Hunter's Tryst and I don't think her Rotary club would approve of Maxine Campbell being portrayed as the hoor of Oxgangs.'

Hawk smiled. 'I can assure you that she'll never darken the doorstep of a brothel, nor tout for business on a street corner. I'll make her a businesswoman with a nefarious side.'

Hawk groaned inwardly. Maxine's alter ego was going to be a crack whore who got murdered, but now he would have to rewrite the first few chapters he'd battered out on the flight from New York. Never mind; he would re-write it. Easy-peasy.

'...sandwich?'

Hawk hadn't been listening to Mrs Moore, and he smiled at her as he caught himself. 'I'm sorry, I got distracted.'

'I asked if you would like a sandwich. They were

specially made by Mrs Wilson. She's one of our organisers.'

Jesus. More Scottish sandwiches. He hoped they weren't cucumber, or even worse, haggis. He couldn't stand the stuff. Yes, he ate hotdogs, and some people thought they were filled with shit shovelled off the floor, but by God they filled a hole when you were hungry and a street vendor had just freshly cooked a batch of Sabretts.

Hawk grabbed a sandwich – ham and cheese. He was having a glass of wine when he was approached by the museum's curator, Donald Masterson, a man who could have been in his late forties but dressed twenty years older. He was leaning on a walking stick held in his left hand.

'Hawk. Thank you so much for graciously coming along here tonight. I truly appreciate it.' He smiled at the writer and held out a wiry hand to shake.

Hawk gripped it with all the enthusiasm of putting his hand into a hole in a tree.

'Good to be here as usual, Donald. I'm so glad you were able to have me along here tonight.'

'Maxine will be over the moon at winning our little auction. She's such a big fan.'

'She's a terrific lady. I'll take good care of her.'

Masterson smiled. 'I'm sure you will.' He patted Hawk on the arm before walking away.

Hawk talked to Maxine about her role in his new book, spoke to each of the twelve guests in turn and signed a book for everybody.

At the end of the evening, when most of the guests had filtered out, a young woman approached him.

'Stella. Glad you could come tonight.'

'Dr Hawk, I hope you don't mind, but I brought the paperback of your last book and was wondering if you could sign it?' Stella Graham smiled at him.

'Of course I will.'

She led him across to where her winter jacket was hanging up and took a paperback novel from one of the pockets. She was still holding on to the hardback that Hawk had signed for her.

'Glad you could come here tonight,' he said to her in a whisper, winking at her.

'I couldn't stay away.'

'I know. I'll see you down at the hotel.'

'Nothing to get nervous about.'

'I'm not nervous. I'm...excited.'

'Me too. Won't be long now.'

He took the book from her and signed it. Handed it back. Stella smiled and put the book back in her jacket.

He watched her as she put her jacket on and walked over to the door. She turned and smiled at him before she left.

TWO

Detective Chief Inspector Sean Bracken put the two glasses down on the table.

'Cheers,' Chaz Cullen said, smiling at him. She took a sip of her gin as Bracken sat opposite.

'Cheers.'

They were in Winston's, a small pub off St. John's Road in Corstorphine. One of Chaz's regular haunts. A place where if they didn't all know her name, they were certainly working their way up to it.

'I was shopping with your favourite pathologist this afternoon and she was asking how I was spending my Saturday night. Not any old Saturday night but Boxing Day to boot.'

'And you told her you were spending it with your favourite detective?'

'I did, but then I said he couldn't make it so I was having a drink with you instead.' She smiled and took another sip.

'Working with all those chemicals in the mortuary has gone to your head.'

She looked around at the other customers; they were mostly older blokes, maybe getting wasted before going back to the wife. Getting out after Christmas Day, burning off the turkey.

'Don't take offence at my words,' she said, the smile still firmly fixed on her face. 'Although I think that should have been your line.'

'It was meant to be an observation.' Bracken sipped his pint.

'You don't seem yourself tonight.'

'I was just thinking about a conversation I had with Sarah when I saw her yesterday. She has a male friend. She likes him. He's on the verge of becoming her boyfriend.'

'What's holding her back?'

'She's not sure. She wants the three of us to have a drink and then I can suss him out.'

'Do you think he's worried that you're a big, bad copper?'

'He'd better be worried I'm big. If he's going to try any pish, he'd better be twice my size.'

Chaz could only imagine how big that would have to be. 'Maybe Sarah knows that this new friend is skating on thin ice when it comes to the police. You know, like he smokes funny wee roll-ups that he'd prefer you didn't know about.'

'Let's hope that's all it is.'

'Don't let it ruin our wee after-Christmas drink.'

'I wouldn't dream of it.'

She looked at him. 'Listen, I know I've only known you a week and we've had a few drinks as colleagues, you being the copper and me being the mortuary assistant, but since you saved my life, I thought maybe –'

Bracken put his pint down gently on the table. 'Chaz, listen, I was only doing my job. I don't want you to think you have to...you know...'

She put on a shocked look. 'I was going to say, you could come along to a party I've been invited to, as my guest.'

'Let me finish. I was going to say, you don't have to invite me to any parties you might be going to.'

'I think I'm going to faint. I've never heard such filth from a man in all my life.' She waved a beer mat in front of her face. 'You know you've pulled a beamer, don't you?'

'I could light my old granddad's coal fire with my face.'

'For a hardened copper, you certainly know how to let a wee lassie like me get the upper hand.'

'A thirty-two-year-old lassie. Still, I should put you over my bloody knee, right here in front of the whole pub.' He chugged his pint, hoping the cold liquid would put out the fire that was spreading across his face.

She laughed at him and put the beer mat down. 'You didn't really think I was offering you...well, you know...'

'Of course not. I was pulling your chain.'

'Liar. But anyway, now that you think I'm the hoor of Corstorphine, the invitation still stands. To come to the Hogmanay party on Thursday night, I mean, not the other thing.'

'Will it be full of impudent wee lassies like yourself?'

'Of course it will. You never know, you might pull.'

'I'm not in the market for a girlfriend right now,' he said.

'I'm a girl, and I'm your friend.'

He thought about it. He'd met her at the mortuary a week ago, after moving back to Edinburgh from Fife. His whole life had moved to Fife after the divorce and he'd started again. A few casual girlfriends in the six years he'd been there. He'd made new friends and only kept in touch with one from the old days, Bob Long, a former detective inspector who owned the small guest house where Bracken was staying until he found a place of his own.

Now, all the friends he'd made were back in Fife and he'd told himself he didn't need any new ones. After all, he could go back and have a pint with them any time he felt like it. But he knew it would never be the same.

Was that why he had spent some time with this younger woman with purple streaks in her hair who had an infectious smile and made him feel happy when he saw her?

His new friend Chaz Cullen. Was that how he would introduce her if he bumped into his old DI? 'Cameron, this is my friend Chaz.' Cameron Robb was one of his closest friends, a man he was definitely going to keep in touch with. He'd already met up with him in the past week.

'Everybody needs a friend,' Chaz said when he didn't answer.

'I know.'

'I'd like to think this is the start of a beautiful friendship,' she said, teasing him again.

'You don't know anything about me,' he said.

'That isn't strictly true.'

He held up a hand before she could go further.

'You know my ex-wife's name is Catherine, my daughter's name is Sarah and I've been divorced for six years.'

'We know that each of us was married and we're currently single. So that makes for the start of a good friendship.'

'Do you hang out with any female friends?' he asked her.

'My ex-husband and I went out as a couple. I had some friends, but I was the married one and they were single. We drifted apart. Now, Pam Green and I go out for the occasional drink.'

'And you saw there was a new detective in town and thought you would rope him in to carrying you home when you get blootered.'

'Yes, because young DS Izzie Khan can't quite manage to swing me over her shoulder.'

They finished their drinks. 'One for the road?' he asked her.

'I'd like to just go home,' she said. 'I know, party animal. But I just feel tired.'

'That's fine. I can walk you home.'

'Considering I live just along the road from you, that isn't as chivalrous as it sounds.'

'I can only try.'

Outside, more snow had fallen, but the roads were

wet and clear. Bracken shrugged into his overcoat and shoved his hands into his pockets. Chaz slipped an arm through his.

They chatted as they walked along the main road then turned into the next street. Chaz lived in the Paddockholm, a little development of modern houses.

'You coming up for a nightcap?' she asked him.

He nodded. 'Sure.' He knew she was still shaken up after what had happened the week before, and she would still be looking over her shoulder for a while, wondering if it really was over.

'I got some beers in. And a half-bottle of Scotch.'

'Does it come with a little brown bag so you can drink it on the bus going to work?'

'And a carrier bag, no less.'

They both heard a scream coming from behind them, and Bracken saw the terror on Chaz's face as she spun round. Her arm was still through his and he felt her grip tighten. He put a hand over hers.

A drunk couple on the main road were having a laugh. The drunken woman was bent over, laughing, and she screamed again.

'It's fine. I'm here,' Bracken said to Chaz.

'Oh, Christ, Sean, is it ever going to end?'

'It will still be raw for a while. Tonight won't be the last time you'll jump at something, but it will get easier, I promise you.'

'You're still coming up for a nightcap?' she said, as if he had lied to her.

'Lead the way.'

Upstairs in her flat, she opened the fridge door.

'Why don't I put the kettle on?' he said to her.

Chaz looked at him for a moment, waiting for the punchline. 'Oh, you mean it?'

He smiled. 'A cup of coffee would be just the ticket right now.'

'Coffee it is.'

'And I won't tell people you asked me up for a coffee,' he said, filling the kettle from the sink.

They went through to the living room, where Chaz put a CD on, starting on track two.

'The Blue Nile,' she said. '*A Walk Across the Rooftops*. One of my favourites.' They sat down on the settee, the music just background noise.

'It's one of my favourites too,' he said as 'Tinseltown in the Rain' played.

Chaz was quiet for a moment. 'I'm having trouble sleeping,' she said to him. 'I wake up thinking he's in the flat here, waiting to kill me.'

'He's dead, Chaz. He isn't coming back.'

'I know that. When it's morning and it's light outside, I know that. But at night, when everything's quiet and it's dark and all I can hear is ticking clocks… that's when I hear him.'

'I know how you must feel.'

'Oh, God, Sean,' she said and leaned against him as she started crying. He put his arm around her shoulders as the music played on.

THREE

Bracken didn't know how long he was going to stay at the Glenfiddich guest house, but Bob and his wife, Mary, weren't in a hurry for him to move on. His first week there had been comfortable, and he knew there would be no point in looking for a place in the run-up to Hogmanay.

It was literally a five-minute walk from Chaz's flat, situated on the main road. It had been a private house many years ago and, like some of the other houses, had been converted into a guest house.

There weren't any lights on, either in the guest lounge at the front or in the rooms above. Bob and Mary's own living quarters were at the back of the house, in an extension.

He was quiet as he let himself in and he took each step with caution, getting to know which stairs creaked.

He felt like he was creeping up the stairs to meet a hoor.

He made it into his room without sounding like an axe murderer. He didn't bother with a light. The room was small enough that he could find his way around in the dark.

He walked over to the window and was about to draw the curtains when he saw somebody out the back.

He moved quickly, glad he hadn't taken his coat off yet, taking the stairs two at a time. His eyes had adjusted to the dark and he could see where he was going. He was careful not to knock over the small table in the hall, the one with the lamp on it, which had been turned off ages ago.

The door to Bob and Mary's private quarters was straight ahead, but the guest dining room was on the left and there was a door in there leading out to the back garden. Somebody hadn't closed the curtains in the dining room and Bracken could see the intruder outside, pacing about.

He took out his extendable baton and tried unlocking the door but found it already unlocked. He opened it, not knowing if the hinges would squeak or not. If they did, he would rush out, all attempts at a covert entrance gone, but to his surprise they didn't utter a sound.

He stepped out onto the flagstone patio. The figure

was facing away from him, dressed in black, just like he was.

'Show me your fucking hands now!' he shouted, flicking the baton open.

The figure stopped pacing and he could see their hands at their sides as they turned round.

It was a woman. She had a cigarette in her mouth and one hand reached up to take it out.

'Do you always point that thing at a woman?' she said. 'And we haven't even been properly introduced yet.'

'Get your hands up against the wall,' Bracken said.

'I don't mean to get off on the wrong foot, but –'

'Sean!' Bob Long said, coming out of his kitchen door with two mugs in his hand.

'Christ, do you always creep about in the dark?' Bracken said. 'I nearly gave you a new set of false teeth.'

'Cheeky bastard. These are all mine. But before you go all Chuck Norris on this lady, maybe I should introduce you. Detective Superintendent Kara Page. Your new boss.'

Bracken looked at his friend, then at the woman with the cigarette.

'Filthy habit, I know, but it's my New Year's resolution to smoke more.' She took a puff and took the mug Bob offered her.

'Kara, this is DCI Sean Bracken, the reprobate I was telling you about.' Bob grinned at Bracken, who collapsed the weapon and put it back in his pocket.

'As introductions go, I can't remember a more memorable one.' He looked at Kara. 'I apologise, ma'am. I just saw somebody creeping –'

'Actually you saw somebody having a quiet smoke while she was waiting for her coffee,' Kara said.

'Please accept my apologies, and I'll leave you to whatever it was you were doing.'

'Don't make it sound mucky,' Bob said, sipping his own coffee. 'The kettle's just gone off if you fancy a brew.'

'I've just had one.' Bracken looked at both of them, hoping that somebody would tell him why his new boss was standing in the back garden of the guest house where he lived.

'You might be wondering why I'm here,' Kara said, taking a final drag on the cigarette before nipping it and putting the remainder back in the packet.

'Aye, well, it had crossed my mind,' Bracken said.

'Let's go into the dining room, if you don't mind, Bob.'

'Fine by me,' Bob replied, and he closed his kitchen door and they trooped into the room.

Bob switched on a lamp. The tables had been set

for breakfast. They sat at one and Bob and Kara put their mugs down on coasters.

'Kara's the replacement super,' Bob explained.

'Aye, I figured that out after you said she was my new boss,' Bracken said. He turned to look at Kara. 'Usually they wait until I get to the station.'

'I'm living here in the guest house,' she said.

'That explains a lot.'

'Sorry for the confusion, but I have a bit of a problem with my new place.'

'Somebody broke in and trashed it,' Bob said. 'Threw paint everywhere, smashed walls, the lot. Bastards.'

'CID are working on it but getting nowhere fast,' Kara explained.

Bracken knew she wasn't from the Edinburgh division, so she must have moved here from another area. 'You're not from around here, ma'am.'

'Correct. I'm a transplant from Inverness. I used to work here in Edinburgh. I worked with Bob and I knew he had retired, so I thought I'd look him up when I arrived. I have a place here that I'd been renting out and just recently listed for sale, so I decided to take it off the market and move back in. It was in good condition until somebody decided to redecorate without using a paintbrush.'

'I worked with Bob too and I don't seem to remember you,' Bracken said.

'I moved around a bit. I was a fast-track candidate and was working undercover on a drugs sting when I met Bob. I didn't meet you.'

'They certainly moved quickly to fill our previous super's shoes,' Bob said.

'I was already being eyed for a position in Glasgow, but they asked me if I wanted to come back home instead. I jumped at the chance.'

'Who would want to trash your house?' Bracken asked.

'No idea. Crime scene were working the place today. I only arrived this afternoon and discovered the damage. If it hadn't been for Bob and Mary having a vacant room, well, to use your vernacular, I would have been fucked.'

'Do you think it's somebody local who knew you were home? Somebody you've had dealings with in the past?'

'Me? Have enemies?' Kara said sarcastically before drinking some of her coffee. 'I've been threatened more times than I've had a Greggs sausage roll. Maybe we should just round up every scally I've locked up and we can pick one out.'

Bracken wondered if she was married, and if she was, where her husband was. He looked for a ring on her finger, but she was holding the mug in both hands and the fingers of her right hand covered the left.

'Are you married?' he asked her, going for the direct approach.

'Bob did say you were a fast mover, but your speed even shocks me.' She gave a slight grin and put her mug down on the table.

'I was wondering if maybe you had a vengeful ex,' he said.

'I know you were. You went into detective mode, and I like that, DCI Bracken. But no, there's no husband. Not for a long time, and I don't think he would class himself as vengeful.'

'I said you can stay here for as long as you want,' Bob said, 'and I meant it.'

'I appreciate that, Bobby.' She put a hand over his before looking at Bracken. 'I owe this man a lot. He saved me and I've never forgotten it.'

'Och, away, Kara.' Bob sipped his coffee while Bracken flashed him a look that said he would be asking about this later over a beer.

'I'm assuming you haven't received any threats recently, or else you would have mentioned that,' Bracken said.

'Nothing,' she said. Bracken didn't believe her.

'No disrespect, ma'am, but my head isn't buttoned

up the back. I've been in this job a long time, I've sat across from many a toerag –'

'Easy, Sean,' Bob said.

'I did say no disrespect. But if there's something we should know about your house getting trashed, then maybe this would be the best time to tell us. I want to help you if I can.'

'Your concern is duly noted, DCI Bracken. If anything comes to mind, then I'll let you know.' Kara stood up.

'Right. Anyway, good meeting you, ma'am, and if you need me for anything, just give me a shout.'

'In the guest house, it's okay to call me Kara. In front of the other guests. At work...well, you know the drill.'

'I'll do that,' Bracken confirmed.

'Good night, folks. Sleep tight. Don't let the bed bugs and all that. See you in the morning.'

She walked out of the dining room, both men watching her departure. She was hiding something and she knew Bracken knew.

'A wee heads-up would have been appreciated,' Bracken said.

'You were out courting Chaz.'

'Courting? For God's sake, you been watching *Upstairs, Downstairs* again? I told you before, Chaz and I have a wee drink because we're colleagues.'

'Whatever. But Kara called me up and told me about her house. The estate agents who were listing it had it cleaned yesterday. It isn't going to be redecorated for a wee while because of the short notice, but it was clean for her to move into.'

'What about furniture?'

'The removal van is on its way down, but it was furnished. Now that stuff has been smashed up.'

'Any idea who did it?' Bracken asked.

'She's not saying anything, but I was a detective and you still are. Between us, we can both see she's feeding us a line. I'm not sure, but I think this was personal. I mean, how many scrotes could know she was coming down here?'

'Somebody at her old station? A boyfriend she just dumped because she was coming down here?'

'Anybody's guess. But you should maybe fire a rocket up the arse of the DI from CID who's landed the case. I'd bet he isn't going to win any medals for closing it. He'll feed her the same crap he's told dozens of people in his career: "There's not much we can do." But make sure he's had the forensics team in. Fingerprints and all that. You never know – after the cleaning crew were in, they wiped everything clean, and the suspect could've left some fresh prints behind.'

'When exactly did it happen?' Bracken asked.

'This is Saturday, and the cleaners were in Friday

afternoon. Kara arrived after lunch today, so within a twenty-four-hour period, Friday afternoon to Saturday afternoon.'

'Where were you between those times?'

'Don't even start. I have an alibi, and if I didn't, I know somebody who would get me one.'

'You say that like you believe it,' Bracken said.

'I do believe it. More to the point, where were *you*?'

'I need an alibi, Bob. Can I say I was with you?'

'Bog off. You're on your own there, son.'

They stood up from the table.

'Maybe you could ask her again after breakfast tomorrow,' Bracken said.

'See? I said you would need me again.'

'I can honestly say, the station isn't the same without you, Bob.'

'I think I've been insulted,' Bob said, opening the door into the back of the house where his and Mary's quarters were.

'You are a good detective after all,' Bracken said, grinning at his friend as he left to go upstairs.

Bob's parting words were something about being careful not to insult the people who cook your food, and Bracken gave some thought to just opening an individual packet of Rice Krispies in the morning.

FOUR

Edwin Hawk stopped outside the Inn on the Mile and alternated between looking at the outside of this building and his hotel just across Niddry Street, a little lane that dissected the two establishments.

A pint or two before bed? Yes, the hotel had a bar, but he fancied a beer with the locals. Even if he didn't strike up a conversation, he could always sit and listen to the conversations others were having – something he often did so he could put their words into the mouths of the characters in his books.

Living in New York, he was at a disadvantage when it came to doing research. It wasn't like he could just hop on a bus and go somewhere to do research.

He was looking back up the High Street towards the castle, for no other reason than that it was there, when he spotted her. Christ, that was all he fucking needed.

He quickly turned away and walked down into his hotel, hoping she hadn't spotted him. He went into the bar, pretending he hadn't seen her. But she had obviously seen him.

'Hello, stranger,' a voice behind him said as the barman took his order.

He turned to look at her. 'Hardly a stranger,' Hawk replied. 'I only saw you yesterday.'

'That was a day ago. I've thought about you a lot since then.'

'There you go, sir,' the barman said, putting the pint of lager on the counter.

Tracey stood looking at him expectantly. *Fuck's sake. Order her a drink and she'll sit with me,* he thought. *Or give her a hint and sit down by myself, and she'll buy her own or walk out.*

As a psychologist, he was used to mentally sparring with people, and this was going to be no different.

'If you'll excuse me, I have to do some note taking,' he said, handing money to the barman, who went to the till and got the change. Hawk turned his back on the woman, sending a second signal: Goodnight, sweetheart.

He took the change, grabbed his pint and headed

over to a table in the corner, not turning to look back at her.

Luckily, he always carried a little notebook so he could jot down ideas or snippets of conversation when he was out and about, so he fished it out of his inside pocket.

'Anybody sitting there?' Tracey said a few minutes later.

'Actually, I'm waiting for somebody.'

She pulled the seat out and sat down, putting her glass on the table. 'No, you're not. You have your wee book out, just like you always did when you were going to spy on somebody in a public place.'

'It's called research,' he said, closing the little book but putting the pen between the pages. Message: I've just put this pen in here as a placeholder so I can continue when you move your ass out of the way. Or maybe he should use *arse* instead. They were in Britain after all.

'It's called eavesdropping.' Tracey took a sip of her drink and put the glass back down. 'You told me that yourself the last time you were in my fair city.'

He had unzipped his jacket and saw that Tracey had done the same thing, but she had also managed to lose one of the buttons on her blouse. He knew some guys would let their gaze wander, but not him. They were doing the dance now and glancing down at her would be letting his guard slip, and that was something he couldn't afford to do, not with this woman.

Hawk had written not just fiction but also a few non-fiction books, on subjects from 'how to handle divorce' to 'how to get through the working day without killing your boss'. All books showing how to use psychology on people.

Hawk certainly wasn't going to produce a hammer and touch Tracey with it, now or in the future. In fact, he was a man who vomited just from looking at photos of dead bodies, never mind physically hurting somebody.

'Look, Tracey –' he started to say, but Tracey held up a hand and he saw the smile slide off her face like a cliff sliding into the sea, taking houses with it.

'This is it now, Ed, is it? Let's have a good time with Tracey, then do a runner?' She picked up her glass again and took a bigger sip. He thought she was going to burst the glass, the way her knuckles turned white.

'I'm not doing a runner, Tracey, because there's nothing to run from.' He smiled at her, making sure to keep looking at her hands in his peripheral vision in case she went for a weapon. 'We talked about this. You said you understood. I believed you, but now you have to prove it. You and I can't be together.'

'It's not like that.'

Maybe he could reach his pen in time if she had a brain fart and couldn't remember where she was for a moment and started throwing furniture at him. Like the last time. Different bar, same psycho.

She took a deep breath and gently put the glass down. 'I'm sorry for what I did the last time, but you hurt me, Ed. Hurt me badly. Spending the night with me and then telling me you were going to leave your wife for me. Next thing I hear, you're happily married still, and I've been dumped.'

Hawk looked at her, wondering if she was on medication now. Trying to get through to her the last time had been like talking to a brick. It'd had no effect, and just given him a headache.

Tracey was delusional, having slept with him only in her own imagination. The lines between reality and imagination were blurred.

Though Hawk could mentally tussle with people, Tracey was starting to make the hairs on his neck stand up.

'I see you're not denying it,' she said, her voice now a whisper, like a sea being sucked away from the shoreline. He knew the tsunami was coming.

But she surprised him by smiling. 'I know it's hard, you working in New York and me living in Edinburgh. Long-distance romances are difficult, but not if we both want it to work.'

He made eye contact with her, knowing that was the only contact he could make. He knew that reaching a hand over to cover one of hers would be like a marriage proposal in her eyes.

'Tracey, I appreciate all of your hard work in promoting my book by word of mouth to your friends, but –'

She put up a finger to her lips. 'Shh, my love. I'm willing to give it another go. I can overlook your little infidelity. You can tell your wife that it's over, that you and I spent the night together and we're going to be spending every night together from now on. Call her now, if you like. Then you can pass her over to me and I'll give her a piece of my mind.'

Hawk didn't move, like he was sitting next to a hand grenade whose pin had been pulled.

'I don't have a phone,' he said after a few moments. 'But even if I did, there would be no point. Tracey, I appreciate you being a fan, but that's all it can ever be.' *Besides, I'm not even married!*

'I know you can't talk about it in public, my love,' she said, interrupting him. 'I'll give you time on your own to process the situation.' She stood up and smiled at him. 'I'll be in touch. Sleep tight, Ed. Sweet dreams.'

He watched as she left by the main door, relief flooding through him. She was a whack job and no mistake. But then the little voice in his head jumped in.

You invited her into your life, Ed. You can't blame her.

He sat and wrote some notes, then looked up at the woman approaching his table.

'She giving you hassle again?' Stella said, coming over to him.

Hawk was glad that she had listened to his advice: If you see this woman, then stay away. She's trouble.

'Yes. She somehow thinks that I'm married, and it seems to excite her to think I'll be having an affair with her. I can't convince her I'm not married.'

'There's always one. Never mind, let's just go upstairs and I can show you how to relax.'

He smiled at her. 'Now that's the best thing I've heard all night.'

FIVE

Bracken woke up when it was still dark, and he wondered who the hell was playing music at this ungodly hour, although he wasn't exactly sure which ungodly hour it was.

Then he realised that his phone was breakdancing across his nightstand and, unlike on TV, he was instantly awake.

He grabbed the phone, looking at the number. He didn't recognise it and promised himself he would hunt them down if it was somebody trying to sell him life insurance. At five-fifteen on a Monday morning.

'Bracken,' he said, answering.

'It's Jimmy Sullivan, sir,' his DI said. 'We got a shout.'

'Control called you?'

'Yes, sir. I wouldn't have disturbed you, but I'm at the scene now with Izzie and it's a go.'

'Text me the details.'

'Will do.'

He disconnected the phone from the charging wire, switched a lamp on, burning his retinas, then turned it back off. He decided to use a small torch he kept in the bedside cabinet for emergencies or a trip to his en-suite through the night after a sesh with Bob.

He switched his little kettle on, took a quick shower and got dressed, the torch balanced on the nightstand, facing the ceiling, providing a muted glow as it bounced off the white paint.

He nearly cowped over putting his leg into his trousers but steadied himself. *Jesus, Bracken, you only had a few. Pull yourself together.*

He finished dressing and made a coffee in his travel mug. It was one thing getting up in the pitch dark in the middle of winter, but it was another leaving the house without adding some caffeine to the bloodstream.

The car took a few minutes to warm up, and he drank some coffee and listened to a radio station while the heat through the windscreen took care of the frost.

He looked at the text from Jimmy Sullivan again; Lady Stair's Close, just off Wardrop's Court. *Park in the Lawnmarket.* From previous visits, Bracken knew

Lady Stair's Close ran through Wardrop's Court and it ran downhill from the Lawnmarket to Bank Street.

Most of the vehicles were there, blue lights flashing, when Bracken arrived. He parked behind the mortuary van.

Coffee in one hand, he showed his warrant card to the uniform who was standing at the entrance to the close.

He walked through the short tunnel that ran through the old tenements above his head. Hundreds of years ago, people would have been throwing buckets of pish out of their windows into this court.

Arc lights lit up the scene, bouncing off the white forensics tent. Inside, Bracken assumed, was their victim.

Sullivan walked over to him, his breath rising in the cold air. He eyed up Bracken's travel mug.

'Keep your filthy eyes off it,' Bracken warned, taking a sip of the hot liquid to reinforce his possession of the mug.

'There wasn't a second cup?' Sullivan replied.

'Do I look like your wife?' Bracken said. 'No, don't answer that. There would be something far wrong if I did. What do we have?'

'Young woman, found dead sitting on the bench. A drunk going home, taking a shortcut through the close, heading for the Mound on the other side. He stopped to ask the victim for a light. Called it in.'

'Man or woman, this drunk?'

'Man. Ian Stevenson.'

'Is he blootered?'

'Was. Seeing a dead woman tends to sober you up pretty quickly. Seeing my wife with her rollers in has the same effect.'

'I hope I never have to witness that.'

'She only wears them through the night. And if you did, I'm pretty sure I'd be filing for divorce the next day.'

'Don't worry, I have no intention of seeing your wife with her rollers in, or any other time.' Bracken took a sip of the coffee as they walked towards the tent. 'Could this bloke have been responsible?'

He knew that some killers would call the police from the scene, pretending they'd found the victim.

'I don't think so. That's my feeling. We'll do backgrounds on him, but my gut says no.'

'Where was he walking to?' Bracken asked, scanning the buildings on all sides of the scene. There were countless windows overlooking the court. A lamppost was in the middle, standing on a low pedestal. The Writers' Museum stood in front of the crime scene, its round turret poking into the night sky, which was threatening to dump more snow on them.

'He said he'd been at a party in the Grassmarket and decided to walk and try to hail a cab, but he came through here to answer the call of nature. He relieved himself round the corner before seeing the victim there. He lives in Broughton Road.'

Bracken looked at the DI. 'He came in here for a pish? Bit brazen, wasn't it? Especially given what would have happened to him had he been caught with his pants down. Literally.'

'It happens to drunks all over the world, I suppose. All pished up and nowhere to go.'

Bracken nodded towards the tent. 'So he walked in and then what?'

'He went over to a corner by the Writers' Museum, finished and was coming back towards the steps here when he saw her sitting on the bench. All alone.'

'And naturally he went up to her, thinking he was in with a chance or something? Pretending to ask for a light.'

'Could be.'

Bracken knew all too well the outcome of such a scenario: young man out for a good time got drunk, got knocked back, then decided to help himself, whether the female was willing or not.

'Is the pathologist in there?' He nodded in the direction of the forensics tent and drank some more coffee.

'She is. With Chaz. You know, the one who's young enough to be your daughter.'

'She's thirteen years younger than me, and we just have a drink now and again. So shut your pie-hole.'

'Just an observation, boss. I wouldn't want you getting yourself in trouble.'

'If this is you giving an opinion when you're sober, then God help us all when you're pished.'

Sullivan smiled at his boss's back as they walked over to the tent. There was a uniform standing guard; the only people who were in the square were polis.

'Knock, knock,' Bracken said, pulling a flap aside.

The generator outside was supplying the power for the little arc lamps within.

'Sean! Glad to see you're up and at it early,' said Dr Pamela Green. She was one of the city's pathologists.

'You couldn't have sprung for a wee heater in here as well as the lights?' Bracken said.

Chaz, standing next to Pam, said, 'Morning, DCI Bracken.'

'Good morning, Miss Cullen. Is this a private party or can anybody join?'

'I think your rank gets you exclusive membership,' Pam said.

Bracken looked at the woman's frozen features, her head tilted down as if looking at her hands in her lap. She was wearing a heavy coat and a scarf was hanging loose round her shoulders. He could see the ligature mark on her neck as he crouched down for a better look.

'You know what questions I'm thinking, Pam, so I'll just stand here drinking my coffee while I listen to your answers and observe the scene.'

'She died here, and it looks like she was strangled with the scarf.'

'No signs of sexual assault?'

'None so far, unless he took her clothes off and managed to dress her again without anybody noticing. And did it perfectly. You know how hard it is to actually dress somebody? I haven't done it since my son was a little boy, but an adult? Even my husband has always dressed himself, hangover or no hangover.'

'This book was on her lap,' Chaz said.

Bracken looked at the hardback, which had been placed in a clear evidence bag. *Enemies All Around*. Edwin Hawk. 'Anybody read any of his stuff?'

'I have,' Sullivan said from behind the big detective. 'He's pretty good. And he's here in town just now, giving some talks. Maybe that's where this victim got her copy.'

'Is it signed?' Bracken asked.

Chaz took it out of the bag and flipped the pages. 'It is. *To Maxine. Best wishes, Edwin Hawk.*'

'I wonder if she was here tonight?' Pam said.

Bracken looked puzzled. 'I'm not the best at riddles, Pam, so maybe you could enlighten this daft old fart?'

Sullivan gave a short laugh behind him.

'I was talking about you,' Bracken said.

'I knew that.'

'Here, as in the Writers' Museum,' Pam elaborated. 'Edwin Hawk was giving a private talk to patrons of the museum tonight. Last night, I mean.'

'Was there ID on her?' Sullivan asked.

'No. Just this signed book.'

Bracken looked at Sullivan. 'See what you can find out about her. Get Angie and Izzie to deliver the death notice when we find a next of kin.' Then he looked at Pam. 'What timescale are we looking at here?'

'No more than eight hours. Around ten or eleven last night.'

'Thanks. I'll see you later today at the mortuary.'

Before he left, Bracken took his phone out and snapped a photo of the dead woman's face. He gave Chaz a smile before he left the relative warmth of the tent. Sullivan followed.

'Anybody who's in and has a window overlooking this square, wake them up. Somebody might have seen something.'

'We've started the door-to-door, but I'll make sure every door is knocked on.'

Sullivan was about to walk away, but Bracken stopped him. 'Everything okay, son?'

'What? Aye, everything's fine.'

'You can go to counselling. Nobody will take the piss out of you if you need to talk to somebody.'

'I'm fine, boss.' Sullivan didn't make eye contact but merely walked away.

Bracken knew events like those of the previous week could get under the skin and sometimes it was good to chat with somebody about things. Bracken had spoken with Chaz. They had talked things out and he'd assured her it would be okay. She was a good friend and he enjoyed her company. More than that? He didn't know where the future would take them, and right now he was taking it one day at a time.

He looked around for Stevenson, who had found the victim. He was standing talking to a uniform – about football, it looked like; anything to keep him from wandering off.

SIX

'Is that coffee you have in there?' Stevenson asked, nodding to the thermal mug Bracken was holding.

'It is. Why? You think it was vodka?'

'Naw, dinnae be daft. I wouldnae mind a wee sip. I'm freezin' here.'

'You want me to let you share my coffee? Put your lips on the lid of my mug?'

'Aye. I'm clean!'

'You told us you had a pish round the corner before you saw that dead lassie there. Where did you wash your hands?'

'It was only a pish.'

'Manky bastard. Your lips and hands are going nowhere near my mug.' Bracken made a face as if he couldn't believe Stevenson would even think about asking.

He took a sip of the coffee. 'Now, I want to ask you if you knew the victim.'

'Oh, so now you want my help. I'm not good enough to share your coffee, but I can answer your questions. Is that it?'

'Or I can have that officer there arrest you for indecent exposure. You admitted to exposing yourself round the corner. There might have been a bairn looking out of one of the windows, and there you are, flashing yourself for everybody to see. You know what they do to men like you in Saughton. Then the judge will make sure you're put on the sex offenders register when you're back out. *Ian the Beast* they'll call you. But that's okay, you don't want to answer my questions here, I can ask you them in the station after you've been processed.'

'Okay, okay, easy there, Inspector. I'm just cold, that's all. Of course I was going to answer your questions. No need to mention the other stuff.'

'So?'

Stevenson looked blank for a moment. 'Oh, aye; did I know her? Naw. Never seen her before in my puff.'

'Was she alive when you first saw her? You know, after you were busy playing with yourself round the corner.'

'Aw c'mon. It was a quick pish. I live down in

Broughton. I used the lav before I left my mate's flat, but the cold gets a grip o' the bladder. Don't tell me neither of youse has had a pish outside before.' He looked between the detective and the uniform.

Both men ignored the question.

'Anyhoo, she was sitting there with some snow on her head. I thought to myself, she must be bloody freezin' out here. I went over to see if she was alright. She had a book sitting in her lap. It had snow on it too. That's when my spidey sense got tingling.'

'You felt yourself tingling?' Bracken said, looking at the uniform. 'I don't know about you, son, but when I see a woman sitting alone on a bench in the dark, I don't get a tingling feeling.'

The uniform slowly shook his head. 'Nor me, sir.'

'See, Ian? Neither I nor that fine young police officer get our baws tingling when we see a woman sitting alone. There's a name for dirty bastards like that.'

'Naw, naw, nothing like that,' said Stevenson. 'You're twisting things about. Not tingling in an excited way but getting the hair up on the back of my neck. I thought something was wrong.'

'You got a tingling feeling when you thought you could nick her handbag?'

'I never touched her handbag! I didn't even see a bag!'

43

'There wasn't a bag on the scene when we got here,' Bracken said. 'Maybe you shoved it up your juke before we arrived.'

'Take a look!' Stevenson said, unzipping his jacket and standing with his hands by his sides, showing his shirt and nothing else.

'You might have emptied it and put it in one of those bins over there. Forensics will be going through them later on.'

'Och, away, man. I just found her and called the polis. I didn't touch her, or her bag. I didn't see a bag. She looked like she'd been sitting there for a wee while.'

'Did you see anybody else around here?'

'I heard voices, but it's the time of year when everybody is out celebrating. I didn't see anybody near the woman.'

'Take a look around you, son. See all of those windows? I'd bet a penny to a pound that somebody was looking out of one of them. And what are they going to tell me? That they saw you talking to that lassie? That she was alive and you were already revved up after touching yourself and you thought she was wanting a go. She was obviously looking for a man who was reeking, because that's a turn-on, when he's staggering about, looking for a place to have a slash, maybe have a wee pavement pizza to himself. Aye, that would make the lassie want to drop her drawers for you, eh?' Bracken screwed his face up.

Stevenson looked at the big detective, his warm breath spewing out with every word he uttered.

'No, Ian, I don't think the lassie was feeling like taking you home with her. She was probably thinking, Jesus, get this drunken bastard away from me; he reeks of pish and alcohol.'

'She couldn't think that, Inspector, because she was deid.' Stevenson's voice had gone soft now, and this time he made eye contact. 'This is why naebody phones the fuckin' polis. Big bastards like you come along, and the next thing you know, some wee plooky-faced hoor is picking you out of a lineup and the shagger who works the legal aid cases comes to the station, not a clue what he's dain, and then you're in a cell, getting a stiff kicking or getting engaged to your cellmate –'

Stevenson's voice had been getting higher and higher, until Bracken put a hand up, smiling.

'No need to get excited, son. I was only asking you some questions. But know this.' The smile suddenly dropped. 'I'm going to have somebody pick your life apart, and if I find out that you were even sucking a sweetie outside a school playground, I'll boot your bollocks so hard, people will think you've got a new dimple on your chin.'

'You're a real polis, aye? I mean, you weren't just walking past and decided to have a wee neb and now you're getting carried away?'

'Oh, I'm the real polis, son. And you don't want to find that out the hard way.' Bracken fished inside his pocket for a business card, still holding on tight to the thermos mug. He found one and held it out for Stevenson.

'You can go now, Ian, but I want you to pop into the West End station to give your statement in writing.'

'Will you be there?'

'No. Somebody else will take it.'

'This isn't a trap, is it?'

'No trap. And if we have to come looking for you, I'll make sure all your neighbours know we're looking for a suspected beast.'

Stevenson snatched the card, looked at Bracken once more and then walked away, heading for the steps that led down to the Mound.

'That certainly put the wind up the wee roaster,' Sullivan said as he walked back over.

'I was just having a conversation with him. He might not have a record, but he's well dodgy. Run him through the system again. More thoroughly.'

Bracken watched Stevenson disappear from view. He knew Sullivan had contacted control and asked for a background on Stevenson, and had there been anything, he would have intervened before Bracken let the man go.

'He just hasn't been caught. Whether he's a murderer or not remains to be seen,' Sullivan said.

'Everybody has a skeleton in a closet somewhere.' Bracken looked at Sullivan. 'As we both found out last week.'

SEVEN

For Edwin Hawk, Sunday morning was a leisurely breakfast. Two bacon rolls, not a full Scottish breakfast, which looked like a heart attack on a plate.

He was just sitting sipping his coffee when the news came on. A woman found dead near the Writers' Museum. Unidentified.

He had been giving thought to a new series, a character who was more rough-cut than his detective hero. Sometimes he felt himself slipping into the role. It would have been more authentic if he had brought his gun over. The illegal one he'd bought, for self-protection. The gun laws in New York State were ridiculous.

'You seem far away, darling,' Stella said, coming into the living room area of the suite, towelling her hair dry.

'A woman's been found dead up the road. Outside the museum.'

Stella sat down. 'Did they say who it is?'

'Probably some drunken broad who slipped and fell. The police are treating it as suspicious, but they haven't given out any more details.'

Stella Graham helped with his research and was boots on the ground when he was back in the States. When he came over four times a year on a research trip, he would hook up with her and they would do the research together.

For Hawk, it usually meant timing how long it would take a character to run from A to B, and things like that.

For Stella, it was a chance to order some expensive things from the room service menu.

'It's got to be more than just the police finding a woman in the snow,' she said.

'It's nothing to do with our talk last night,' he said. 'Everybody left together and we went our own way in the High Street.'

She smiled at him. 'Don't tell me that the crime writer in you isn't thinking that one of you doubled back and killed somebody.'

'Don't talk like that.'

'It's true.'

'We don't even know who it is yet.'

Stella finished her coffee as Hawk started to put things in his messenger bag.

'I won't be long getting dressed, then we can go,' she said.

'I just have to send a quick email before we go out on the town,' he said to her.

Stella took the lift down and stepped outside into the cold morning air. Maybe it was all in her imagination, but it didn't seem as cold down here as it did in her hometown of Kirkcaldy. Maybe she just didn't feel the cold when she was over here with the love of her life.

She had never seen Edinburgh like this before, even though she worked here in her normal job. Being in love made her see the city through the fabled rose-tinted glasses.

A few minutes later, Hawk came out and they jumped into a fast black.

EIGHT

Bracken rolled his sleeves up and watched as DS Angela Paton came in with a bag of rolls.

'Cheese for Izzie, and bacon for everybody else,' she said.

'Here, take this,' Bracken said, handing over some money. 'This is on me.'

'Thank you kindly, sir.'

They were sitting at their desks, a coffee in front of them, and they unwrapped the rolls and tucked in.

'I have to say, I'm tapping the mat here,' Sullivan said. 'I'm usually still wrapped up under my duvet at this time on a Sunday.'

'You're going soft, sir,' Izzie said.

'Were you out on the lash?' Bracken asked.

'Over at the nursing home seeing my dad. The boys were running about wild.'

'Sorry to hear that, son.'

Sullivan shrugged. 'He's been ill for years. He can't look after himself now, and we didn't go on Christmas Day because my sister went then.'

Bracken felt there was more explanation needed but didn't pry.

Then the door to the incident room opened, and they all looked surprised to see the woman standing there, except Bracken.

He got to his feet. 'Everybody, I'd like to introduce our new boss, Superintendent Kara Page. Ma'am, this is my team. Or your team, as it were.' He introduced them all.

She stepped further into the room and took her coat off. 'I was due to come in tomorrow to meet and greet you all, but this woman being killed last night has brought things forward.'

'Coffee?' Bracken asked, kicking Sullivan's foot. Sullivan walked over to the machine and waited.

'Thank you. Just milk. But please, sit down. I'd like to listen in.'

'I'm sorry, I didn't get any extra rolls,' Angie said.

Kara waved her away. 'I've already eaten.'

Sullivan made the coffee and they sat down.

'Right then,' Bracken said, washing his roll down with his coffee. 'Have we managed to get hold of Donald Masterson?'

Masterson was the curator of the Writers' Museum and the emergency key holder.

'He's on his way in from Penicuik,' Izzie said. 'He's been there all night. He got a bus home, he says, after the book reading.'

'Good. I want to meet him over there. Maybe they'll have CCTV.' Bracken looked at Sullivan. 'Anything from the door-to-door?'

'Nothing concrete. Lots of squeals, screams and laughing. It's like that every Saturday night, apparently.'

'Get a team to go back in case some people were out. And do we know the whereabouts of this Hawk joker? The writer?'

'As you know, Dr Green said he was doing a wee talk at the museum last night, but she doesn't know much more than that,' Sullivan said.

'I want to speak to him. If we can't find out where he is, maybe Masterson knows where he's staying,' Bracken said. 'How did we get on with next of kin?'

'Nobody seems to know anything about her. We can't find an address. No hits on the fingerprints. There's nothing to go on right now.'

'Keep on it. Her family might not live in Edinburgh. There was obviously a lot of footprints in the snow, so we don't have anything from that.'

'Who found her?' Kara asked.

'A young man on his way home taking a shortcut through the close,' Bracken answered. 'I questioned him on the spot, and we have his details. He's coming in to give a statement.'

'Did you get any vibes from him?'

'I think he was just in the wrong place at the wrong time.'

A phone rang on one of the desks and Angie answered it. She spoke for a few seconds before hanging up. 'That's Donald Masterson in the museum now.'

Bracken stood up. 'Good. We'll get along and have a word. Jimmy, grab your coat.'

'I'll come along too,' Kara said. Nobody objected.

Downstairs, in the small car park, Bracken leaned close to Sullivan. 'Try to drive like you've actually been behind the wheel of a car before.'

'I can't promise anything.'

'I can promise you something,' Bracken replied, 'and it involves having a steel toecap being surgically removed.'

'I'll sit in the back,' Kara said, as if Sullivan's reputation had preceded him.

The drive was relatively quiet, Bracken observing that the drunks and ne'er-do-wells were all tucked up in bed. The nightcrawlers would be back out in force after dark.

'How was crime in Inverness?' Sullivan asked Kara.

'About the same as it is here but on a smaller scale.'

Bracken thought Sullivan was itching to ask why she had transferred south, but the DI kept his mouth shut.

They parked where they had parked earlier in the morning, but daylight made a difference now. A weak, watery sky was above the square, waiting to dump snow at any time.

Bracken took the lead with Kara following as they showed the uniform their warrant cards. Through Lady Stair's Close and down the steps to the square itself and across to the Writers' Museum.

The scene was still marked by police tape and the forensics tent was there. People in white paper suits were doing their thing.

'You ever been to the museum, ma'am?' Bracken asked, nodding to the old building with its door on the corner and a turret way above.

'Once, a long time ago.' She looked at him. '"Feare the Lord and depart from evil."'

Sullivan looked blank.

'It's engraved on the lintel,' Bracken said and they looked above the door. 'Ignoramus,' he added under his breath, looking at the DI.

Bracken tried the door handle but found the door

locked. He knocked on the wood, and they waited a few minutes before it was answered by a man who looked like he had seen a ghost.

'Come in, quickly,' he said, as if the killer was standing right behind them. He moved awkwardly, holding on to his walking stick.

They filed in and Masterson slammed the door shut, causing them to turn round.

'There's a killer out there and here I am, waiting for the police to come and interview me. Here, in the building not ten steps away from where somebody was murdered.'

He was a thin man with wispy hair that he may or may not have been trying to coax into a comb-over. Without much success. He wore wire-framed glasses and had an exaggerated blink that made Bracken think the lenses weren't helping. He leaned on his walking stick.

'I slipped on the ice and partially dislocated my right knee,' he said when he saw Bracken looking at it. 'I have a brace on. I'm scared to be out walking in this snow now.'

'But you made it out last night for the Edwin Hawk do.'

'Oh, yes. I never miss one of those. Come through to the main hall,' Masterson said, and he led them into the room where the literary talk had been given the night before. 'This is a terrible business,' he said. 'Just terrible.'

'We'd like to ask you a few questions,' Bracken said. Noting how warm it was inside, he asked, 'Is the heating always on?'

'Of course it is. We have valuable exhibits in here. Did you know we have Rabbie Burns' desk here?' A slight smile moved his lips as if the murder had been momentarily pushed aside. 'And the printing press that Sir Walter Scott's novels were made on.'

'And a ring given to Robert Louis Stevenson by a Samoan chief,' Sullivan said.

'Engraved with the word "Tusitala",' Kara added. 'Which means "Teller of Tales".'

'You're both fans of Stevenson then?' Masterson said, almost foaming at the mouth.

'No,' Sullivan said. 'There's a poster in a frame there with the story.'

Kara nodded to confirm that she too had read it when they came in.

Bracken thought Masterson might have used the term *fucking heathens* if he hadn't been so polite, and he sensed any forthcoming offer of a coffee was now on a hiding to nothing.

'About last night, Mr Masterson,' Kara said, bringing the conversation back on track. 'You had a literary talk going on, is that right?'

'A little soiree with a few invited guests, yes. Edwin Hawk is a favourite of ours. Such a nice young man. He's American but comes across to Edinburgh a few times a year on research trips. His books are set here.'

'We need to know who was here at your wee shindig last night,' Bracken said.

'It was hardly a ceilidh, Inspector. There was no drunken rampage going on and I would very much like it if you didn't start suggesting that, thank you very much!' Masterson pointed to a poster on the wall of Edwin Hawk holding a copy of his latest book. He appeared to be a small man and was standing next to a table piled high with his books.

'Please, we're not trying to suggest anything inappropriate was going on,' Kara said, jumping in.

'As well you shouldn't, young lady. We had a nice little get-together with an author who's always very accommodating when he's here and I won't have anything bad said about him.'

'Not even if he's killed somebody?'

'Och, away and don't talk such tosh,' Masterson said, and Bracken thought he'd said *pish* at first as he struggled to keep his teeth in.

'We need the names, if you don't mind,' Kara said.

'Okay, fine.' Masterson fished a notebook out of his pocket and showed it to Kara, who took a photo of it. Names and phone numbers.

'I want to show you a photo of a woman,' said Bracken. 'But I have to tell you first that she's dead. Could you look at it for us? It doesn't matter if you can't.'

'Oh, dear. I'll try, if it will help you, but I don't have a strong stomach for that.'

Bracken brought his phone out and showed Masterson the photo he'd taken of the victim earlier out in the courtyard.

'Good God. I can't be certain, but that looks like Maxine. Oh Lord.'

'Maxine?' Bracken said.

'Maxine Campbell. She was here last night. She won the bid at our little auction to have her name used in a new book by Hawk. Oh, that's terrible.'

'Do you have any details for her?'

'Not personal details. I just met her through Hawk.'

'Did you leave alone last night?' Kara said.

'No. I locked up, but there were a couple of stragglers. Helen Moore and one other woman. We walked to the bus stop down on South Bridge together.'

'We need to speak to Edwin Hawk. Do you know where he's staying?' Bracken asked.

'Down the road at the Radisson Blu.'

They thanked him and left the museum, stepping into the cold, sharp air.

'What do you think about this Edwin Hawk?' Kara asked.

'He looks like he couldn't tear a wet paper napkin in half, never mind kill a woman,' said Bracken. 'What about you?'

'Same.'

'But never underestimate somebody,' Sullivan added.

'You've got a point there. Some small guys go for it.'

'Talking from experience, DCI Bracken?' Kara asked.

'I am actually. Some of those wee bas...fellas look on it as taking home a trophy if they knock a big guy out.'

'How come all the big guys want to fight me?' Sullivan said as they walked through the close back to the car.

'Oh, I don't know,' Kara said, 'I've only known you five minutes and already I feel like punching you in the face.'

Sullivan looked across the roof of the car at Bracken as Kara got in the back. Bracken made a face and shrugged his shoulders.

You're on your own, pal.

NINE

They parked behind the taxi rank on the High Street and Sullivan put the police sign on the dash. He had spoken to Angie Paton on the phone and told her to try to track down a next of kin for Maxine Campbell.

'This is a posh place,' Kara said, eyeing the Radisson Blu hotel.

'A little bit bigger than Bob and Mary's,' Bracken admitted. 'But you don't get the same company you get in Glenfiddich.' Bob had named his hotel after the whisky he had been drinking that night, with the approval of his wife.

'That's true. It's good to see Bob again. Mary too,' Kara said.

Bracken reckoned that Kara was going to enjoy their company while she was living there.

They went inside and approached the reception.

'Is Edwin Hawk in his room?' Bracken asked as they all showed their warrant cards.

'I saw him go out a little while ago,' said the man behind the desk.

'Can I speak to your manager?'

The man picked up the phone, spoke into it and hung up. 'He'll be with you shortly. Can I get you anything while you wait?'

'Why? Is he going to be that long?' Kara asked, staring at the man.

'No, he's just coming. He's just finishing up something.'

'Give me the phone and dial that number again.'

He looked at her for a moment, like he was about to ask if it was a joke, but she just waved her fingers a couple of times.

He handed the receiver over and hit a button.

'I just told you, I'll be there in five minutes, for Christ's sake. Don't you think I've got better things to do than stand about chatting?'

'This is Superintendent Page. Let me assure you, you do *not* have anything better to do than be out here with us. Not if you value your career. I'm looking at my watch right now, and when I hang up, you have until the second hand does a full sweep, then we will walk out of here and I will be making another phone call to somebody way higher up the food chain in your hotel. You're a small cog in a big machine, Mr...?'

'Kent. I'll be right there.' He hung up before she did and she looked at her watch. Twenty seconds later, a small, wide man was standing in front of them.

'Sorry about that. I thought he was winding me up again. He's always pranking me.' Kent looked over at the receptionist. 'Any more of that and it's your jotters,' he said, laughing.

Bracken was sure there were obscenities going through the receptionist's mind, but he didn't voice them.

'Perhaps we could go through to the bar?'

'I don't drink, Mr Kent,' Kara said.

'They serve coffee and tea as well as alcohol.'

They went through and were seated at a table.

'Coffee,' she said. 'No sugar.'

Bracken and Sullivan asked for the same, but Sullivan wanted sugar in his.

'I'm trying to cut down, but it tastes like God-knows-what without it,' he explained once Kent had gone.

'Jimmy's trying to get in shape so he can have the same physique as me,' Bracken said.

Kara shook her head. 'Next time you try weight-lifting, Bracken, put some weights on the end of the bar.'

Bracken raised his eyebrows at Sullivan, promising a kick in the goolies if he laughed.

Kent came back, sweating, like he'd just run through to the kitchen to order the drinks himself. 'It will be here shortly. I told them we had some VIPs in the bar.'

'Sit down, Mr Kent, you're making the place look untidy,' Bracken said.

Kent sat down and took a cotton hanky from a pocket and wiped his forehead. 'I'm sure the heating's on the blink. I'm sweating like a P.I.G.'

'Yeah, it is hot in here,' Bracken said, and his eyes shifted over to the draft handles, where a nice, cold pint of lager was waiting on the other end.

A waitress came over with a tray with four cups on it, and the condiments.

'I'll be right back with the coffee pot,' she said, smiling, as she retreated.

'Thank you,' Kara said.

'Now, we need to ask you a few questions,' Bracken said.

'No bother. Fire away.' Kent looked at the ceiling for a second before answering.

'Edwin Hawk, the writer, is staying at your hotel, we believe,' Bracken said.

'Yes. Nice man.'

'We're not interested in whether he's nice or not,' Sullivan said.

'Oh, right, then in that case he's a mouthy American who could do with being taught a few lessons in manners. When he gets a drink in him, he's that loud, the fishermen in Aberdeen can hear him.'

'Does he ever get violent?' Kara asked.

'Violent?' Kent looked at her like she was daft. 'Far from it. Don't get me wrong, he's loud and annoying, but he spends money like he's just printed it. He's very generous with the tips too, which is a complete one-eighty from all the other bloody Americans we get here. They're so tight, they make Hawk look like Rockefeller.'

'Was he in here last night?'

'Yes. He was telling me earlier in the day that he was going to a wee shindig up at the Writers' Museum. He came in here afterwards.'

I'm not the only one who thought of it as a shindig. Bracken brought his phone out as the young waitress brought the coffee pot and began pouring. He waited until she was done before opening up the photos, watching as Sullivan poured the milk and added two packets of sugar to his own cup.

'Do you know a woman called Maxine Campbell?' Bracken asked Kent.

'Maxine Campbell? Yes, I've seen her hanging around Hawk. Is she...?' Kent made a face.

'Dead? Yes.'

'Jesus. What happened to her?'

'We're not at liberty to say. And I'll have to ask you to keep that information to yourself.'

Kent shrugged, not impressed with the lack of gossip.

'Did you ever witness anything untoward between Hawk and this woman?' Kara asked.

'Like what?'

'Like arguing or fighting.'

'Oh no, nothing like that with Maxine. Not like that other troublemaker. Her name's Tracey Pitman. She's been in the hotel every night asking for Hawk. He was drinking in the bar with her one night.'

'Why is she on your radar?' Kara asked.

'She's loud too. Not as loud as he is when he's had one too many, but she seems...volatile. One minute they were having a drink, and the next she jumped up and started shouting at him.'

'When was this?'

'Before Christmas. I thought she was another groupie, but then she left and we didn't see her on Christmas Day. She was in last night. I thought she was going to start on him again, but she sat down and then left shortly afterwards.'

'They weren't fighting?' Bracken asked.

'No. He didn't buy her a drink. She bought her own, sat at his table, and didn't stay long. Then the other woman joined him.'

'What woman?'

'His girlfriend. They just left the bar and went up to his room.'

Kara nodded. 'You have her name on file, I take it?'

'Of course.'

'We'll need it. And we need to get in touch with Hawk. I assume he left an emergency contact number in case you have to get hold of him when he's out.'

'I'll go and get those details for you now. Enjoy the coffee.' Kent got up from the table and left.

'Is Hawk married?' Kara asked.

'I was looking at him a bit online,' Bracken said. 'He's single. There's no mention of a wife or kids. It stands to reason he would have a girlfriend.'

They drank some of the coffee and waited for Kent to get back. Bracken felt like he had been up for days. He started thinking about going to the party with Chaz, not sure if he wanted to or not. They were friends, and some of her other friends might misconstrue things. He didn't know if he was ready for that yet. But he wanted to be around for her, after what they'd been through a week ago.

Kara was looking at her phone. 'Hawk seems to

have written quite a few novels. He sets them here in Edinburgh. Strange place for an American to set his books. I wonder why he chose here?'

'He worked here as a psychologist for three years,' Bracken said. 'It's in his bio.'

'Then that makes sense. I wonder where he was before Maxine died.'

'He has an alibi with his girlfriend,' Sullivan said.

'Love makes us do daft things,' Kara answered. 'I should know.'

TEN

'Detective Finn McCloud and his trusty dog, Skootch, are walking alongside the Water of Leith. They walk under the St. Bernard's Bridge, just along there.' They were standing in the little corner area of Kerr Street and Saunders Street, and Hawk pointed down the road. 'What do you think?'

Stella thought that she couldn't feel her face anymore and she wished she was wearing furry knickers. There was a bench and a Christmas tree had its lights on, but the cold was nipping at her, so she really couldn't concentrate. She was here with Hawk; that was the main thing.

'Fabulous idea, Hawk. I love it.' And she did love it, but getting a tour of Stockbridge was starting to lose its appeal.

He turned and smiled at her. 'So they walk under the bridge and come up here, heading for home. Then Skootch comes here, into this little corner. It's called Jubilee Gardens. Did you know that?'

She smiled back and shook her head. 'No, I didn't know that.'

'Skootch wants to come in here for a pee – maybe against the tree, I haven't decided yet. But when they come in, they find a body at the base of the tree. And that's the start of Finn's case.'

He beamed a smile. There was nothing new in his description, nothing that would make her swoon if this were a 1930s movie.

His phone rang. 'Who could this be?'

'You won't know unless you answer it.'

He smiled and wagged a finger. 'Hello?'

'Edwin Hawk?'

'Who's asking?'

'My name is Detective Chief Inspector Sean Bracken of Police Scotland. We need to have a talk with you. Can we meet up?'

'I'm in the middle of some research right now.'

'It's about a murder we're working on. We can meet with you or we can have somebody bring you to the station for a formal interview.'

Hawk looked across the street and saw a café.

'Caffè Nero, Glanville Place, down in Stockbridge. It's on the main drag.'

'We'll be there. Meet you inside.'

Hawk hung up and looked at Stella. 'It's the police. They want to talk to me about a murder. I'm assuming the one we saw on the TV.'

'You? Why would they want to talk to you about it?'

'I have no idea.' He looked across at the café again. 'Come on. I need a stiff shot of Jack Daniel's, but coffee will have to do.'

'You know I don't want to go home tonight, don't you?' Stella said to Hawk. 'But I have to or else he'll just try to make trouble.'

'I know, honey. Soon you won't have to worry. But we don't want him on our radar just yet. He thinks you stayed with your friend, and he knows you help me with research, but we don't want to get his hackles up. We'll be together soon enough. Not that he could stop you staying with me.'

'I know, but I want things to be peaceful until we go.'

They were sitting in the café when the unmarked patrol car pulled up outside. Hawk watched their every move, with his little notebook sitting on the table.

'Taking notes?' Stella asked.

'Yes. I want Finn to be the best private detective there is. He's going to be interacting with the police.'

'Your bank account tells you that he is.' Stella reached a hand over and put it over his.

ELEVEN

The three detectives walked in, looked around and walked over to Hawk.

'Detective Bracken. Let me get some more coffees in.'

Kara was about to argue, but then thought that they were using the café's facilities so it was only fair that they bought something.

'Okay,' Stella said.

'My DI will get them in,' said Kara.

Sullivan turned away and walked over to the counter to put the order in. Bracken and Kara sat down at the table.

'You wanted to talk to me, you said,' Hawk said, a smile on his face.

'We want to talk to you about Maxine Campbell,' Bracken said.

The smile slowly fell off Hawk's face. 'She's dead, isn't she? She's the one at the museum. The one who was on the news.'

'How do you know that?' Kara asked.

'I write detective novels. I might not be a police officer like you guys, but I know a lot about police work. She's dead, isn't she?' he asked again.

Sullivan walked over with two coffee cups for his colleagues and went back for his own before sitting down.

'Yes, she's dead,' Bracken answered.

Stella put a hand to her mouth. 'Oh my God. She was at the reading with Hawk last night.'

Hawk looked at her like she'd just thrown him under the bus.

'I saw her leave,' she added quickly. 'She left the museum on her own. I was with Hawk all evening and he didn't leave my side all night.'

'Somebody killed her and left her on the bench at Lady Stair's Close,' Kara said.

'God almighty,' said Hawk. 'That's awful.'

'How well did you know her?' Bracken asked.

'I've known her for years. She was a big fan. She came to all my readings and book signings in Edinburgh. We also worked together in the Royal Edinburgh before I left.'

'And you got on well with her?'

'Oh, yes! She was great.'

'What about Tracey Pitman?' Kara asked, sipping her coffee, which was superb. 'We heard she caused trouble for you in the bar in the hotel.'

'You don't know Tracey like I do. You see, she's a fan of mine. I get a lot of letters from fans and I enjoy talking to them, but some of them take it too far. You know, they get jealous when you talk to another fan and don't give them enough attention. I see it happen all the time. That's why it's important not to lead them on or give them false hope.'

'What did Tracey want from you?' Kara asked.

'To be my wife.'

Stella looked at him before looking at Kara. 'She put him through the mill.'

'You're Mr Hawk's girlfriend?' Bracken asked.

'Yes,' she answered, and Bracken noticed Hawk's cheeks tinge with red, as if he was embarrassed to admit it.

'Stella has to finalise some things before we can be together properly. As in, so we can get married. Then we can both move to America.'

'You currently live in New York, is that right?' Kara said.

'Yes. I moved back there six months ago after working here for a few years. I got offered a good job working in a hospital in Manhattan. I want Stella to come with me, but she has to finalise her divorce first. We can get her over on a K1 visa. Fiancée,' Hawk explained for those in the room who weren't aware of what it was.

'Tracey didn't know about you?' Bracken asked Stella.

'Oh, yes, she did. That's why she was making a play for Hawk. She wanted me out of the way so she could move in.'

Hawk said, 'It's particularly hard since...'

'Since what?' Bracken asked.

Stella looked at Hawk, silently asking him to answer.

'Since she was one of my patients,' Hawk said.

'I thought you said she was one of your fans?'

'She was both. Patient first, fan next. I was treating her and she got better, so she was released. Then she started writing to me, but under a false name.'

'How long before you left for America did you release her?' Sullivan asked.

'It was only about a month, then I left for New York. About seven months ago. She was one of my last cases. She made good progress and I was satisfied that she could start seeing somebody as an outpatient. She was on meds and everything seemed fine.'

'Can you tell us why she was in the psychiatric hospital?' Bracken asked.

'It was reported in the news, so yes. I'm telling you nothing that isn't public knowledge. She was setting fires. She burnt down a few barns and it was felt that she needed to be put in the psychiatric hospital rather than prison.'

'Who was the doctor who gave her the initial evaluation?' Kara asked.

Hawk hesitated. 'Me.'

'You pronounced her unfit for trial and then you set her free. I read you worked here for three years, so how long after you started working here did she become your patient?'

'Six months, give or take.'

'She wasn't there long then,' Bracken said.

'Two and a half years. There was a catalyst for her actions, which I can't talk about, but I helped her get through it.'

'Do you think there was transference?' Bracken asked.

'What's that?' Sullivan asked.

Hawk looked at him. 'It's when a patient starts to have feelings for their doctor.' Then he addressed Bracken. 'I wasn't getting that vibe. I know it happens, but not in this case. She started getting possessive when I wrote to her as a crime writer.'

'Didn't you think that would set her off?' Kara said.

'The opposite, actually. I was a friend and her

previous doctor, so I felt she would benefit from having a friendly face to talk to, as it were.'

'Did she come along to any of your book signings?' Sullivan asked.

'Yes. She came to all of them on this last tour. I was just doing Edinburgh and a few surrounding cities, but she was at them all.'

Bracken's phone rang and he took it out and answered it. He listened to the caller and the others were all quiet, as if they were listening in.

'Everything alright?' Kara asked when he hung up. Code for, *Tell us who you were talking to.*

'The mortuary. The pathologist wants me to go down there.'

'Are they preparing for the post-mortem?'

'Not yet. It's going to be done tomorrow, with two of the team there.'

'Why do they want you there now?'

'Dr Green didn't say. I'll need dropped off.'

'That's fine.' Kara stood up and looked at Hawk and Stella. 'We'll be in touch again. Don't leave town.'

'Not until next week,' said Hawk. 'I have a job to do while I'm here. Sorry, confidentiality prevents me from discussing it. But I'll be here until after New Year.'

TWELVE

'Her name's Maxine Campbell,' Bracken said to Dr Pamela Green. The smell of the mortuary was competing with the smell from the coffees Chaz had just made. They were sitting in Pam's office and Bracken couldn't help noticing it was eerily quiet.

'How did you get an identification on her so quickly?' Chaz said.

'You mean you weren't earwigging when I was talking to Pam?'

Chaz tried for her most innocent look before sipping the coffee.

'We were having a chat with the curator of the Writers' Museum. Her name was on a list of guests.'

'Where is Maxine's ID?' Chaz said. 'Taken by the killer to make it harder to identify her – but not impossible, with the book. Just buying him time.'

'You too should come and work for me on my team,' Bracken said, enjoying his coffee.

'We've been around enough coppers to know the score.'

'You'll know how to run rings round me in an interview room,' he said as the women smiled.

'We could show you a few moves when you next have to interview somebody,' Chaz said.

'If it involves having to paint my fingernails and threatening somebody with an emery board, I'll pass.'

'Oh, it would involve a move that only a woman could make,' Pam said cryptically.

'You two are scary, you know that?'

'We do,' Chaz said.

Pam put her mug on the desk and picked up a folder. She opened it and looked at her report.

'At the scene I told you that the victim was strangled. We got her naked for a preliminary exam before the PM and I noticed a mark on the palm of her left hand. She was stabbed with something cylindrical. I was thinking what sort of weapon it could have been. Ice pick? Screwdriver?' She looked at Bracken. 'Guess what the weapon was?'

'A sword.'

'You're being ridiculous,' Chaz said, making a face at him. 'Guess again.'

'Did you get it right?' he said to her, raising his eyebrows.

'Of course I did, silly billy.'

'Well, if you can get it right –'

'Now now,' she said.

'I'm kidding. But let me see. It happened outside the Writers' Museum. Something to do with writing, and a quill wouldn't be suitable, so...'

Chaz drummed her fingers on the desk. 'Clock's ticking, Detective. There are only a few days left in this year and your chances of getting the number-one spot on the list for Detective of the Year are getting slimmer by the minute.'

'I'm going to say –'

'And time is up for the big man,' Chaz said in her best TV announcer voice. 'What a shame, just as he was about to pull his hair out, the bell goes and he's out.'

'Go on then, the suspense is killing me,' he replied. 'I know you're dying to tell me.'

'A pencil.'

'Crap. I was going to say that, but I didn't think it was the right answer.'

'You go home with the booby prize, a toy sheriff badge and a stick of liquorice.'

'You'd like that, eh? Me getting the booby prize.'

'Of course I would, Bracken.'

Pam looked at him. 'I was rooting for you to win.'

'Thank you, Pam. It's nice to know I have a friend in here.'

'Just so you know, when she gets pulled over and is about to get a speeding ticket, she's going to name-drop,' Chaz said.

'Fine by me,' Bracken said, finishing his coffee. 'Name-drop away, Pam.'

'What about me?' Chaz said.

'You didn't have my back. You insulted me and humiliated me in front of your colleague, and if this had been a bet, you'd have bet against me. Hang your head in shame, Chaz Cullen.'

She laughed. 'You need a tissue to wipe your eyes?'

'You'll be greetin' when *you* get pulled over.'

'She hardly uses her car these days anyway,' Pam said.

'It's this city. They're choking it. Every rat run has been closed off. Besides, I'm going to get a new bike next year. When the snow's away.'

'That will last five minutes,' Pam said.

'Just you wait and see.'

'A pencil you said?' Bracken said, bringing the conversation back on track.

'Yes. A very sharp pencil. The lead hit a bone, leaving a little bit of graphite behind.'

'That's the conclusion she drew,' Chaz said.

They both looked at her.

'Too soon,' she said.

THIRTEEN

'I decided to take you up on your offer,' Ed Bracken said.

Bracken was driving along to Haymarket and his West End offices and had made the mistake of answering his phone thinking it was somebody else.

'What offer was that, Dad?'

'God, I was only talking to you on Christmas Day. Attention span of a poodle.'

Bracken knew his father loved his German shepherd and looked down on poodles, although to the best of his knowledge, he didn't think his father had ever been dissed by the breed. He heard barking coming down the line, or through the air, whatever technology made him hear his father and the dog.

'You haven't brought Max, have you?'

'Of course I haven't. He's with my pal Mickey.'

'Why didn't you put him in a boarding house?'

'And have him mix with the riff-raff of those sparklers who go to the dog park just to chitchat with their pals and leave their dogs to go humping or fighting? Remind me when I see you later to give you a bar of soap to wash your mouth out.'

'Where are you staying? And why in God's name didn't you give me a heads-up?'

'Well, you just said I should put Max in a boarding house, and I didn't, but that's where I'm going.'

Bracken thought about it for a moment. 'Christ, don't tell me you're going to –'

'Bob and Mary's? Yes. The way you bummed it up, I thought it sounded quite good, so, long story short, I called Bob Long and he said it would be fine for me to come across for a week.'

'What about that party you were going to?'

'With those old cronies from the senior centre? Half of them will be deid by the time Hogmanay rolls around.'

'You're a bloody old crony! I thought you were going out with Mickey?'

'Aye, well, Mickey decided that he's not going. His daughter is coming up from London to see him. That gave me the idea of coming across from Fife to see my wee laddie.'

'Look, it's not that I don't want you around, but we just got a case dropped on us, Dad.'

'Well, I'm here now. Mickey's taking Max for the week. He's feeling a bit down after losing his wife. Max will be good company for him.'

'You know I don't really mind you coming over, but it's busy right now.'

'Don't worry about it, son. I'll amuse myself. But listen, when can you come and pick me up? I'm at the bus station. It's a nice new place. Better class of jakies nowadays.'

'Dad, I'm driving to the station right now. Not the bus station but the police station. Where I work. Get on a tram to Haymarket, and then you can get a bus along to Corstorphine. Get off at the zoo. Don't go in, mind, or they might keep you there.'

'Cheeky wee sod. Where do I get a bloody tram?'

'Look to your left. Up a bit. That's where they stop.'

'Oh aye, I see it now. I'd better get away before some prossie wants to make me an offer I can't refuse.'

'Like steeping your falsers in a glass for you.'

'False teeth are coming for you too, Sonny Jim.'

'I'll see you later on. Try to behave.'

'Of course I will. And you can introduce me to that new lassie you've met.'

'What new lassie?' Bracken said.

'Don't get all coy with me, son. Just introduce me.'

'You'd better make sure you've showered and put on clean underwear.'

'Why? It's not like I'm going to shake her hand one minute, then drop my troosers the next. See you later.'

Bracken disconnected. What the hell was Bob thinking, saying his dad could stay for a week? Christ, this was going to be fun. Bracken loved his dad, but visiting the old sod now and again was fine. He just hoped the old man didn't have an ulterior motive.

FOURTEEN

Everybody was waiting at the station. Bracken yawned as he climbed the stairs to the incident room. Just as well he hadn't been blootered the night before.

'Coffee?' Izzie asked him.

'No, thanks. I'll be getting the shakes if I have any more.' He looked around. 'Where's Super Page?'

'She nipped along to the ladies'. We were waiting on you getting back from the mortuary.'

He took his coat off, thinking about his old man, suitcase in one hand, radge dug in the other. It was just as well he'd left the shepherd at home. People might think he was a beggar. Max would die for his old man and Bracken had seen the big dog go off his nut at the drop of a hat.

Kara Page came back into the large room.

'Right, there you are, DCI Bracken. How did it go?'

He thought for a moment that she was talking about his old man and the dog but then quickly realised she meant at the mortuary.

'The victim, who we now know is Maxine Campbell, was strangled but was also stabbed with a pencil. In the hand, like it was a defensive wound. There was some graphite left on a bone inside her.'

'You think it was a spur-of-the-moment killing?' Angie Paton asked him.

'Not sure. Edwin Hawk has an alibi for immediately after the talk in the museum. Some people walked out with him to the Lawnmarket, and they walked down the road a bit with him and left him at the North Bridge. A few minutes after the time they said they left him, he was seen entering the hotel, so he didn't go back and kill Maxine. But somebody did. Was that person in the group last night? Did she fall foul of a stranger who just happened to kill her for a reason we've yet to establish?'

'We need to find out where she went after the talk in the museum,' Sullivan added. 'It's like she left the square but for some reason came back. And unfortunately met her demise.'

Kara sat on the edge of a desk. 'We need to find Maxine's belongings. Anybody checked with forensics after their sweep of the big rubbish bins in the square?'

Izzie put her hand up. 'I called them and they said

nothing of interest was found. Nothing belonging to Maxine Campbell.'

'The killer took her stuff with him,' Bracken said. 'We need to track down Tracey Pitman as a priority. She was seen arguing with Hawk in the hotel bar a few nights ago, then she was talking to him again last night. Maybe she was hanging outside the museum, waiting for him, saw him talking to Maxine and killed her out of jealousy?'

'We can try to track her down,' Izzie said.

'Hawk has been back living in America for six months, but he told us that Tracey was released on his testimony a month before he returned to the States. She's been out for seven months. Plenty of time to get her little fantasy going in her head.' Bracken explained about her latching on to Hawk.

'Is she stalking him or something?' Angie asked.

'It would seem that way. Hawk thinks that maybe Tracey is in love with him. In her eyes, they should be together. Personally, I think he released her too early. She must be a good actor to convince him she could be let back into society.'

Izzie had been busy typing on a computer. She turned to Bracken. 'Maxine Campbell has a husband,' she told him.

'Get hold of him. Tell him we need to speak with him.'

'He'll be expecting us,' she replied.

'How so?'

'He reported her missing an hour ago at Oxgangs police station.'

FIFTEEN

The Campbells lived in Howe Park, a street in the Hunter's Tryst area of Edinburgh. This was a modern development with detached houses mixed with detached bungalows; the Campbells had one of the former.

Bracken looked along the street to the view of the Pentlands. Still covered in snow, still gave the impression he would freeze to death if he attempted hiking up there.

'That wind shoots right off those hills and slaps you in the face,' Sullivan said, closing the driver's door and locking the car.

'Nice view, but it comes with a price attached right enough,' Bracken answered.

'You going to Angie's Hogmanay party?' Sullivan asked Bracken.

'I haven't been invited.'

'Maybe she's testing the waters. Like she wants to see if you'd be up for it before inviting you.'

'There's only one way she's going to find that out.' Bracken looked at the DI. 'She'll have to ask me.'

'She and her wife are having it at their house. They just moved in. It's a new townhouse on Craigleith Road. Her wife's minted.'

'Sounds like it. I'll wait and see if I get an invite, but if I don't, no big deal. I already have another invite anyway.'

'Oh aye? Care to share?'

'I most certainly do not.'

'I won't be going to the party. We can't find a babysitter.'

The door sprang wide open before they had a chance to knock and a man with dishevelled hair stood before them. He looked to be in his twenties, so maybe not the husband. Bracken never assumed anything, though.

'We're looking for Brian Campbell,' he said.

'That's my dad. Come in. Have you found my mum?' The man was talking fast, like some people did when they were nervous or had something to hide.

He closed the door behind them and they stood in the hallway. He looked at them for a moment.

'Danny, who's at the door?' a voice shouted from further within the house.

'It's the police.' He made it sound like, *It's the polis, hide the stash!*

'Show them in! Bloody halfwit.'

Danny screwed up one half of his face, clearly not pleased with the moniker his father had given him.

'This way,' he said, his voice lower now. 'He's been on edge since my mum didn't come home last night,' he explained.

Bracken knew that calling your son a halfwit didn't happen overnight and thought the boy had probably been verbally abused for a long time.

'Have you found her?' Campbell said as the detectives were shown into the living room. Clean, tidy, but had a lived-in look to it.

'Can you sit down, Mr Campbell?' Bracken said.

Campbell sat. Danny stood in the doorway.

'Leave us alone, Danny,' his father said.

'If it's about Mum, I want to stay.'

'We'll talk about this later,' Campbell said, looking to the detectives now. 'Where is she?'

'I'm sorry to have to tell you, but a woman was found dead this morning and we believe it to be your wife, Maxine Campbell,' Bracken said.

Campbell sat silently while his son screamed and ran through to his room.

'Are you sure it's her?'

'We're pretty certain. We'll need formal identification.'

'How did she die?'

Bracken looked at Sullivan for a second before answering. 'She was murdered. Her body was found in Wardrop's Court.'

Campbell's head snapped towards Bracken. 'Where that fucking museum is?'

'Yes, the Writers' Museum.'

'Did he touch her?' Campbell said, jumping to his feet.

Both Bracken and Sullivan stood up quickly. 'Who are we talking about?' Bracken asked.

'That American. That bloody writer, Edwin Hawk.'

'We don't have any suspects yet, but it would seem that Mr Hawk has an alibi for the time Mrs Campbell died.' He looked at Campbell and put a hand out, indicating that the man should sit back down. When he did, they followed suit.

'She was obsessed with him, you know. All she ever talked about was Edwin Hawk this and Edwin Hawk that. She worked with him in the Royal Edinburgh. Maxine was a social worker, but she's an avid reader and couldn't believe she was working with Hawk. One of her best friends is on the Rotary committee and they had the council run this little book reading thing in that museum. And with us being members of the Rotary, she got an invite along. There was also an auction to have your name used in his next book. Maxine almost mortgaged the house and she won.'

'I'm assuming she found out at the reading that her name had been chosen?' Sullivan said.

'No, she was told in advance. They wanted to make sure the winner was present when the name was drawn. All the bits of paper would have her name on them. All she had to do was act excited and surprised.'

'Did Hawk choose the name in advance?' Bracken asked.

'Not choose, but the name of the highest bidder was revealed and he knew who the winner was last night.'

'Was anything inappropriate going on?'

'I'm just jealous, that's all. I don't know if anything was, but she fawned over him.' Campbell looked at both men. 'He could have killed her, somehow. I'm sure of it.'

'Don't take this personally, but we want to eliminate you and Danny from the inquiry, so where were you both last night?'

'I understand. We were both at the Rotary club; Danny likes a girl there. We were there till around midnight. We were a bit the worse for wear: I came home and crashed out and Danny puked on the rosebushes again, and we went to our own rooms. Then, when I woke up, I noticed Maxine wasn't home. I was more worried than angry, and when I couldn't reach her by phone, I went down to the police station to make a missing persons report. The officer said they would have to wait forty-eight hours before starting a search. I've been calling and leaving messages on her phone, but obviously there was no reply because she's dead.' His voice caught in his throat and Bracken was certain then that Maxine's husband wasn't the killer.

'We can take you down to the mortuary just now, to make the formal ID,' Bracken said.

Campbell nodded. 'I'll get my jacket.' He got up and left the room.

'Hawk didn't say that Maxine acted like an excited wee schoolgirl,' Bracken said. 'Maybe he took advantage of her.'

'If she was a social worker, I'm sure she had her head screwed on.'

Campbell came back in the room and stood waiting, like they were going to the pub. They left the house, without taking Danny.

SIXTEEN

Ed Bracken was entertaining the troops when Bracken got in for dinner.

'There he is, my wee laddie,' Ed said as Bracken came into the guests' living room.

'How was your shift today?' Bob Long asked him.

'Och, leave him alone,' said Mary, his wife, as she came in behind him.

'Long and tiring,' Bracken confirmed.

'On a Sunday too,' Ed said. 'I take back everything I said about you.' He raised a glass of whisky in his son's direction.

'You're starting early, aren't you?'

'It's never too early for a wee swally with the staff of life, son. Here, sit down and join us.'

'I'd love to, Dad, but I have to get ready to go out.'

'Where are you going?'

'I'm meeting Sarah tonight.'

'My wee granddaughter,' the old man said proudly.

'Not so wee anymore.'

'You know what I mean.'

'I do.' Bracken turned to Mary. 'I won't be in for dinner.'

'Okay, Sean. I won't set a place for you.'

Bracken knew he should make more of an effort to spend some time with his dad. Although he had seen him for a wee while on Christmas Day, he had to admit he had tuned the old man out some of the time. It was the way Ed treated him, like he was still fifteen.

'I'll catch up with you later, Dad.'

'I'll be in my bed by nine.'

'Tomorrow then.'

'You out gallivanting until late or something?'

'No, you're just going to bed early. I'll be having a wee drink with Sarah. I'll pass her your love.'

'I'd love to see her while I'm here. Catherine too.'

'I'll tell Sarah you'd like to have a coffee with her.'

'Or something a wee bit stronger.' Ed smiled at Bob.

'We can get you an espresso,' said Bracken.

'Is that some kind of new lager?'

'Yeah, that's what it is. Catch you later.'

He left the living room and went upstairs and showered, feeling the tiredness grip him. Or maybe he was just trying to avoid his old man. Either way, he walked back downstairs and slipped out quietly.

SEVENTEEN

Bracken watched the woman walk towards him and thought he hadn't seen a more beautiful woman in a long time. He remembered a time when she would run to him and he would pick her up and swing her round, making her laugh and squeal.

He loved her like no other woman on the planet.

'Hello, Dad,' she said, smiling at him.

'Hello, Sarah,' he replied, standing up from the table. It still seemed surreal that she was coming into a pub, old enough to drink alcohol. And who was the lanky streak of piss hovering around near her? A young guy with enough gel in his hair to grease the fifth wheel on a truck. He had designer glasses and his clothes didn't seem to have been bought in Oxfam.

Bracken was a big man, and he didn't waste any

time putting himself between the scruffy bastard and his little girl.

'What you having to drink?' he asked her, praying it would be orange juice or something.

'Vodka and coke. And this is Mark, my friend. Can we get him a drink too?'

Bracken turned to look at the scrawny reject.

'Hello, Mr Bracken, sir,' Mark said, smiling and holding out a hand. He accent was very posh, like he should have been at Eton not in Edinburgh.

'Pleased to meet you, son. What you having?'

'I'll have a lager, please.'

'Pint it is.'

Bracken ordered the drinks and waited at the bar as Sarah and Mark stood off to one side. He took his phone out, opened up the camera app as if he was checking his messages and snapped a photo of Sarah's friend. Then he and Sarah sat down as Mark went to use the bathroom.

'Seems decent enough,' he said.

'He's just a friend, Dad,' his daughter said, smiling at him across the table.

'I thought you said you wanted him to be your boyfriend?' Bracken took a sip of his lager and almost bit the glass in frustration.

'It's heading that way. He's a real laugh.'

'He doesn't live with you and your friends, does he?'

'No, of course not.'

'What's his last name?'

'Dad, please don't run him through your system, or whatever it is you do to people.'

'I want to know all about him, sweetheart. It's my job as a dad.'

'Turner.'

'Where does he live?'

'Round the corner from us. He shares a flat with two other students.'

'Do you have classes with him? Is that how you met?'

'No. I met him in here with his pals one night and we hit it off. He comes round to my flat all the time and we go out from there.'

Here was The Argyle pub, just around the corner from where she lived at the moment.

'Has your mother met him?' Bracken said, feeling alarm bells go off in his head.

'Not yet. I wanted you to meet him before she does. You know what Mum's like; she's judgemental.'

'She looks out for you.'

'I don't need her looking out for me. I'm twenty-two next year. I'm a big girl.'

'Christ, Sarah, she's your mother. We're both going

to worry about you.' It came out angrier than he'd intended.

'You know, all this time I couldn't just call you up when I wanted to see you, because you were living over in Fife, but now that I can, you just show negativity. I just wanted you to meet my future boyfriend.'

He could see there were tears in her eyes and he reached a hand out to her, but she pulled away.

'Don't, Dad.' She stood up. 'Why did you have to get divorced anyway?'

'Work got in the way of my personal life.'

'And so it is again. History repeating itself.' She shook her head as Mark came back.

'See you around,' she said, and motioned for Mark to follow her out, which he did, leaving his pint untouched. He smiled and waved over at Bracken.

Some of the regulars were watching him but saw nothing was going to happen, and they went back to drinking.

He didn't feel guilty about what he had said to his daughter. She was the love of his life, and something wasn't sitting right. She didn't know where the piece of piss lived, but Bracken would find out.

He took his phone out and called his old DI back in Fife, Cameron Robb.

'Cameron, old son. It's me, Bracken. Listen, I'm

sorry to disturb you on a Sunday, but I have nobody else I would trust with this.'

'You don't have to apologise, boss. I told you before you left, you need anything, give me a call.'

'I appreciate that, son. I just had a meeting with my daughter and she brought along some yahoo, and get this: the prick is about to become her boyfriend. She wants to take it to the next level. But she doesn't know where he lives. I have a gut feeling –'

'Say no more, boss. Just give me his name.'

'Mark Turner. He looks maybe twenty-five but could be a bit older. Talks like a toff, but he sounds like he's putting it on. And I could swear I've met him before.'

'Maybe you've lifted him in the past.'

'That's what I'm wondering myself.'

'I'll get on to it soon, then get back to you.'

'Thanks, pal.'

Bracken hung up and took a last sip of his lager before leaving the warmth of the pub.

He turned right and walked along Warrender Park Road to a little pizzeria just off Marchmont Road. He took his phone out and thought about calling Sarah, but instead he dialled another number.

A man answered. Bracken remembered how he'd felt just a week ago when a man answered Chaz's phone. How'd he felt thinking she had a boyfriend.

'Roger, it's Sean.'

'Oh, hi, Sean. You'll be wanting my sister?'

'That's why I called her number, my friend.'

'Roger! I've told you not to answer my bloody phone!'

Bracken heard Chaz shouting in the background. Words were said as Roger evidently handed over her phone.

'I only know one Sean,' Chaz said. *'I'm assuming it's the one who carries a warrant card. Otherwise, no, I don't want a warranty for my car.'*

'Pity. I could get you a good deal on a warranty,' Bracken replied. 'Otherwise, how does pizza sound? I'm starving. I skipped dinner so I could meet Sarah.'

'Sounds good. I didn't eat dinner either. You want to give me the edited version of how badly it went or wait till you get here and give me the director's cut?'

'This one is going to include outtakes. How did you know it went badly?'

'You told me you were meeting her at seven, and it's not even seven-thirty, yet you're talking to me asking if I want pizza. Call it women's intuition.'

'Spot on. We might have to heat it up, but I'll get a taxi. I might have to wait on it getting made.'

'I'll be here. I'll even have the kettle on.'

'No, you hang up,' he said.

'You hang up, or I'll put Roger back on. The man who's just leaving.'

'See you in a wee while.' He hung up and went into the pizza place.

He didn't see the driver in the van watching him.

EIGHTEEN

'Oven or microwave?' Chaz asked as she took the boxes from Bracken.

'Microwave. I need to eat now. I almost scranned a slice in the taxi.'

'I'm glad you didn't. Take your coat off and I'll heat it up. The pizza, not your coat.' She grinned at him as he shook his head.

She disappeared through to the kitchen, where he heard her pottering about with plates. 'I have the kettle on,' she shouted through.

'Magic.' He went through to the kitchen to make the coffees. He liked the flat. It was in a nice location, it was modern and it was a decent size.

'I'm sorry things didn't go well with Sarah. Sometimes it's hard for a girl to introduce a man to her dad. Especially you.'

'What do you mean by that? Should I be offended?'

She laughed. 'You're built like a brick shithouse. He was probably quivering in his boots.'

'Quite the opposite. He was very confident. A toffee-nosed wee snot, but he had confidence. I clocked that right away. I've met so many of them over the years. He was different, though; he was almost over-confident. But still feral.'

'Like a ferret or something?'

'No, a badger. Or a cat that was born in the wild.'

'Dearie me, Sean. You do know that no man is ever going to be perfect for your daughter?'

'Somebody will sweep her off her feet one day, but I think she brought this mutant along to wind me up. You know, a wee bit of punishment for divorcing her mum.'

'How can a young man who talks posh be seen as a wind-up?'

'Like Daddy has money, so this kid walks on water. Not like Sarah's dad, who's a filthy copper.'

The microwave dinged. 'I have paper plates I keep for special occasions. Like when I can't be bothered washing dishes.'

'I like your logic.' He poured while she put the pizza on the disposable plates.

'I seriously don't know how you can eat pineapple

on a pizza,' he said when they were sitting at her table in the living room.

'It's called a Hawaiian,' she told him.

'I know what it's called. I just don't know how you can eat it.'

'Says the man who has tuna on his half.'

'I like this. The guy in the pizza shop did look at me funny, though.'

'You look like you could rip somebody's arms out of their sockets sometimes.'

'Really?'

'Yes, really. It's the mean copper in you.'

'I always go for the kind, charitable look.'

'It's not working. Except when you're with me.'

He smiled at her. He felt comfortable with her, even though he'd only known her for a little over a week.

'You read a lot, don't you?' he said after chasing a piece of pizza down with some coffee.

'I do. Can you tell?'

'I see the books on your bookcase. Crime novels mostly. Some horror in there. Some old James Herbert.'

'Oh, I love James Herbert. I was gutted when he died a few years ago. One of the best horror writers out there. And Shaun Hutson. I love reading. I immersed myself in books after my divorce.'

'Have you read any by Edwin Hawk?'

'Our victim had his latest book in her lap. I haven't bought that one yet, but I've read the others. For an American, he knows his way around Edinburgh.'

'He lived and worked here for three years before moving back to the States a few months ago. He's just back here on tour.'

'He's a very nice man. I saw him at the Edinburgh Book Festival a couple of years ago.'

'He does give off the vibe that he's a nice guy,' Bracken admitted. 'But it got me thinking: he's a writer. He would use a pencil sometimes, yes?'

'You think he killed Maxine Campbell?'

'He seems to have an alibi, but there's just something not quite right. He was Tracey Pitman's doctor when she was locked away in the Royal Edinburgh. He oversaw her release, deeming her fit to be a part of society.'

'What was she in for?'

'Arson. She wasn't mentally stable, and I'm telling you this in confidence, of course...'

'Of course. And now she's throwing herself at him.'

'She trusts him. Probably the only man in the world she trusts. That's why she fell in love with him, and I think she's having a hard time being rejected by him.'

'She's another suspect.'

'I'm going to have the team track her bank account

tomorrow. Find out where her phone is. See if we can find her that way. She has no friends that we know of, her father has nothing to do with her, and her mother and stepfather are both dead. She has to be somewhere. Unless she goes near Hawk again. I want him to call me so I can speak to her.'

'Do you know what her last address is?'

'She's not at it. We're trying to find out if she has another place she can go to.'

'Edwin Hawk probably knows,' Chaz said, wiping her mouth with a napkin.

'I'll call him tomorrow. Meantime, what DVDs you got?'

NINETEEN

'I hope my dad wasn't any trouble last night,' Bracken said at breakfast.

'Oh, don't be daft. He was no trouble at all. He and Bob were having a laugh and a few nips,' Mary said.

'He's pushing seventy now and he should be taking it easy.'

Ed Bracken stood in the doorway to the dining room. 'A few years away from seventy, thank you very much. I'm known as a classic, not an antique.'

'Earwigging. That doesn't surprise me.'

'Mind if I join you at the table?'

'Be my guest.' Bracken indicated for his dad to take a seat. Then he addressed the others in the room. 'For anybody who hasn't yet met him, this is my dad, Ed Bracken.'

'Hello, Mr Ed,' young Rory McDonald said. He

was sitting with his mum, Natalie Hogan, who had gone back to using her maiden name after the divorce.

'Nice to meet you again,' Natalie said, smiling. She looked across at Bracken and gave him a little smile. When he was working his first case back in Edinburgh last week, he had saved the little boy's life, and Natalie had said more than once that she didn't know how to repay him. She was down on her luck, working in Tesco stocking shelves. She had once been a GP but had been struck off after getting hooked on prescription painkillers.

The old couple who were living in the guest house, Mr and Mrs Clark, weren't down for breakfast yet.

'Did you meet the Clarks?' Bracken asked his father.

'Oh yes, I met them last night. Josh is a great guy. Lori too.'

Josh and Lori. In the week that Bracken had lived here, he'd only known the old couple by their last name. His father had been here a day and knew everything there was to know.

'How was your wee drink with Sarah?' Bob said, smiling as he came in with a plate. Full Scottish breakfast for Ed.

'It was good. I swear she's getting more like her mother every day.'

'Thanks, Bob,' Ed said. 'How's your heid this morning?'

'Surprisingly, still in one piece.' He smiled, still holding the pot holder. 'Mind the plate's a wee bit hot.'

'Cheers, pal.'

'What are you doing with yourself today?' Bracken asked his father.

'I might take a wee trip into town. Why? You offering to take a day off and show me around?'

'I don't think so. I have a killer to catch.'

'Never let work get in the way of a day out.'

'Now I see why you retired without a pension.'

'Don't talk crap. I've got a good pension.'

Bracken lowered his voice. 'Mary has a washing machine and she'll do laundry for a little extra. Don't be washing your skids in the shower.'

'I washed them in the sink along with my socks and dried them on the radiator.'

'Tell me you're joking.'

'Nothing wrong with wanting to wear clean clothes. That way, I only needed to pack three pairs of each.'

'God. I thought you'd have had to put them in a hazardous waste bin. Or at the very least, burn them in the back garden.'

'Don't be bloody clever.'

Bracken laughed and finished his cereal. 'Right, I

have to get ready for work. Try to behave. You have my mobile number. Only call if it's an emergency.'

'Or if I need a lift somewhere.'

'Emergency.'

Kara Page came in and poured some cereal into a bowl.

'Good morning, Kara,' Ed said.

She turned to face them. 'Oh, good morning, Ed. Sleep well?'

'I did, thank you very much. You?'

'Well, I eventually dropped off. You kept me up later than I normally go to bed.'

'I'll give you the money I owe you later on. Have to go to the ATM.'

'That's okay. I know you're good for it.'

Bracken looked between one and the other. Kara turned back to the table and poured some milk from a jug.

'Full Scottish?' Bob said, coming into the room.

'Oh, no thanks, Bob. Just a light breakfast for me when I have work.'

'There's fresh coffee in the pots. Press that bell on the table if you need anything. It's Wi-Fi and we'll hear it through in the kitchen.'

'Will do,' she said, taking her cereal across to a table after letting on to Natalie and Rory.

'I can't believe I'm hearing this,' Bracken whispered to his father. 'If you've been messing about with my boss, you'll answer to me.'

'Shut your cakehole, you wee brat. This belt doesn't just hold my trousers up. We were playing poker. I lost. Your boss is a very intelligent woman. Don't go playing cards with her. Or try your hand with her.'

'For God's sake. I'm not interested in either of those pastimes with my boss.'

'Good. Now, lend me some dosh. I'll pay you back when I get my pension.'

'Aw, Jesus. Don't be betting your house.'

'Don't worry, your inheritance is quite safe.' Ed smiled at his son. 'Or is it? Maybe I'll leave my fortune to Max.'

'A manky old pair of skids and some VHS tapes I could do without.'

'Go ahead, mock if you must. You've forgotten about the hoard of family treasure that I keep hidden.'

'I'm not listening to your drivel anymore. I have better things to do with my time than wonder where you've hidden your Blue Peter badge collection.' Bracken stood up from the table.

'Will you be home for dinner?' Ed asked.

'Depends how busy we are. Why?'

'I thought we could go for a wee drink along the

road. You could bring that lassie you told me about. What's her name again? Chas? Short for Charlie.'

'Chaz with a zed. Short for Charlene.'

'Sounds the same,' Ed said, starting to tuck into his breakfast.

'So does nob and knob.'

'Oh here, behave your bloody self. I'm only showing interest in your love life.'

'She's a friend. We have a drink sometimes. Nothing more to add.'

'Rubbish.'

'As I used to say when I was in uniform, move along now, folks, nothing to see here.'

'So it's a maybe on the pint tonight?'

'Maybe, Dad. But it's a week night and I don't get blootered on a work night.'

'Aye right. Since when?'

Bracken looked quickly over at Kara, who had her phone out and was looking at it while she ate. He leaned in closer to his dad.

'Why don't you shout it a bit louder. I don't think they heard you along at the Gyle Centre.'

'Sorry. I shouldn't have said you were an alky.' He made a zipping motion across his closed mouth and flicked away an imaginary key.

'You'll wish I would throw away the key.' Bracken straightened back up.

Ed laughed. 'I'll make sure I've showered and laundered a pair of underpants.'

'Launder them in a bath of acid. Catch you later. Don't get into trouble.'

When he was in the hallway, Bracken's phone rang. It was Cameron Robb, his old DI.

'Cameron, how you doing, pal?'

'I was up at the crack of dawn. Two things. That guy you asked about, Lord Snooty? He has a record. Lamped a polis when he was drunk, a couple of years ago. Got a fine.'

'Maybe I've seen him around the station.'

'Second thing. You need to get yourself across to our side of the water. An old abandoned house was set on fire last night. There was a woman tied to a metal chair inside and she was burned to death. Unrecognisable, but she had a driving licence stuffed down her throat. Bring your team.'

TWENTY

Kara Page chugged back the remnants of the coffee in the disposable cup provided by Mary Long. Bracken pulled in behind a patrol car.

'Word has it that we'll be getting a new DC soon,' Bracken said to her as he shut the engine off.

'They're moving quickly on this. Your team needs another member and they're going through the applications they had on file. They've narrowed it down. It will be soon.'

The pavements had a white blanket of snow over them. The biting wind, blowing up the hill from Kirkcaldy Bay below, tried to kill them as they exited the car. Kara's hair blew about. Bracken kept his short, so he had no such problem.

Two fire engines were still at the scene, as were patrol cars.

A tall young man walked over to them.

'An abandoned house, you said,' Bracken said to him. 'Ma'am, this is my old DI, Cameron Robb. Cameron, my new boss, Superintendent Page.'

'Pleased to meet you, ma'am.'

'Likewise.'

'This is a house,' said Robb. 'It was part of Fife College. That building in the back is called the Round House. This is the Priory. This is where the fire was set.'

'Vandals?' Kara asked.

'No. There's a lot of rubbish in front of the house, as you can see, left by fly tippers, and there's builders' rubble. There seems to be everything here from old chairs to old mattresses. The Round House back there has been plagued by vandals, but this place was boarded up and relatively untouched. Somebody made his way in at the back, we think, as there are missing boards, unburnt. The fire was set in what might have been a living room many years ago.'

They walked across the snow-covered car park where the fire engines were.

'Any other casualties?' Bracken asked.

'No, sir. Just the victim. The fire was reported at ten-thirty last night by one of the homeowners over the hill there in the estate. It was well alight by the time the fire brigade got here, and they're based not far from here.'

There was a lot of activity around the main door into the old house: a forensics team in white suits, firemen checking for hot spots. The fire commander was on the scene and Robb approached him.

'Sir, this is Superintendent Page and DCI Bracken, Edinburgh Division.'

'What brings you to this neck of the woods?' the commander said. 'Wait – don't I know you?' He was looking at Bracken.

'I was with Glenrothes MIT until last week.'

'Yes, thought so.'

'What do we have here?' Kara said.

They were in the living room, which was a blackened shell. The metal chair was in the middle of the room.

'The victim has been taken to the mortuary, but she's just a burnt husk now.'

'Could your men see it was a woman by the time they got here?' Bracken asked.

The commander shook his head. 'No. She'd had an accelerant poured over her. Petrol. Completely covered, and she was charred by the time we got here. The room was well alight, but this is the seat of the fire. If you see what I mean.' He pointed to the metal chair, which was now warped.

'Who saw the driving licence?' Kara asked.

The commander turned round and nodded to a man who was approaching with a clear bag in his hand. There was an object inside. A pink card.

Bracken pulled on a pair of nitrile gloves and took the licence out and Kara stood close to him as they read it.

'Christ. It says here it's Stella Graham.' It showed a photo of the woman they'd spoken to yesterday with Edwin Hawk.

'It was found shoved right into her throat, which protected it from the fire,' the tech said.

Bracken nodded to him and ushered Robb over. 'Where's that address?'

'Not sure exactly. Ask the commander.'

Bracken did.

'Dysart Road? It's not that far from here, opposite Ravenscraig Park.' He gave Bracken directions after seeing his blank look.

Bracken thanked him and they left the house.

'You want me to come along with you, sir?' Robb asked.

'That would be handy.'

Robb shouted one of his sergeants over and told him to take charge. 'Follow me in your car,' he said to Bracken. 'It's not that far, and I have navigation just in case.'

They got in and followed him along the road. 'I'd be totally lost here,' Kara said.

'I've been here more times than I care to remember,' said Bracken, 'but I'm not sure of the street names.'

Five minutes later, they were pulling up outside Stella's address. It was a semi-detached bungalow, well-kept at the front. On the other side of the road, a low stone wall and trees separated the houses from the park.

They climbed the stone steps and walked along a short path. The front door was recessed and some more steps led to the door. Bracken was about to knock when the door was flung open.

'What fucking time do you call this?' a big man said, then stopped when he saw it wasn't who he was expecting.

'Police,' Bracken said as he, Robb and Kara showed their IDs. 'Who would you be?'

'Tom Graham. I haven't done anything.'

'Are you related to Stella Graham?' Kara asked.

'She's my wife. Why?'

The detectives exchanged looks. 'Can we come in?'

Graham stepped aside and they went into the warmth. He showed them into the living room.

'Stella Graham is your wife, you say?' Kara said to the man.

'Aye. What's wrong?' Graham looked at the three of them in turn.

'You want to sit down?' Robb said.

'Naw. I'm fine standing.'

'We've found a body and we believe it's that of your wife, Stella Graham,' Kara said.

'Stella? Dead? How can that be?'

'She was discovered this morning,' Bracken said.

'Jesus. How did she die?'

'All we can say is, she was murdered. I'm so sorry,' Kara said. 'We have to ask you this: where were you last night around ten-thirty?'

Graham blew out a breath. 'I was in the pub all night with my pals. From around seven to just before midnight when we got kicked out.' He looked at her. 'Was it that American ponce?'

'If you mean Edwin Hawk, we don't have a suspect yet.'

'She was seeing him on Saturday night. She was staying with a friend after some do they were at. She does research for him when he comes over. If he killed her, I'll –'

Bracken held up a hand. 'Take it easy, son. Remember who we are.'

'Aye, well, just you make sure you know where *he* was last night.'

'We'll need the name of the pub,' Robb said.

'Weavers, in the town.'

Robb nodded and wrote it down.

'Will you be expecting me to take a deek at her in the mortuary?' Graham said, screwing his face up.

'We're going to need dental records,' Kara said.

'Jesus.'

'Can I ask you, did your wife work full time for this Hawk writer?' Bracken asked.

'Naw. She was a psychiatric nurse at the Royal Edinburgh.'

TWENTY-ONE

Bracken and Robb drove in opposite directions as they left, Robb going back to the crime scene. He promised to keep Bracken in the loop about the post-mortem and that he'd have one of the other detectives check out Graham's alibi at the pub.

'A love triangle?' Kara said as they headed home.

'We've both seen cases where the husband found out the wife was playing away from home and it ended badly.'

'That could be the case here. If somebody is covering for him, or if he's just outright lying.'

Bracken said, 'Let's see what Edwin Hawk has to say for himself.'

Kara's phone rang and she excused herself and answered it, looking out of the window as Bracken sped down the A90. She hung up and Bracken pretended he hadn't been listening to the conversation; he hadn't caught much anyway.

'That was quick, I have to say.' She looked at him. 'Your wish is being granted. A new member of your team. He interviewed this morning, they liked what they saw and he'll be with us next week.'

'Where's he coming from?'

'He was CID in Leith. DC Mackenzie Brogan. Twenty-nine years old, married with one child.'

'Glad to have somebody starting.'

'You're not the new boy in class anymore.' She smiled at him. 'But then again, neither am I.'

They drove back quickly and Bracken made a call while he was going over the Queensferry Crossing.

'Angie? I'm in the car and you're on speaker. Have Sullivan and Izzie got back from the PM yet?'

'No, sir, not yet.'

'I want you to track down Edwin Hawk. Have him come to the station for an interview. If he doesn't want to come, arrest him on suspicion of murder.'

'Will I say who he's suspected of murdering?'

'I don't want to give a name over the phone. Just see if you can find him. We won't be long.'

'Will do, sir.'

He looked at Kara. 'Messing about with a married woman and taking her to America indeed.'

'You sound like you don't approve.'

'I don't.' He looked at her for a moment. 'I was in Tom Graham's position once. I was working long hours and my wife couldn't resist temptation. She slept with one of her bosses. That was the end for me. I mean, I couldn't blame her for getting bored, but no matter how bored I was, I would never have succumbed to temptation.'

'Never?' She seemed amused.

'Not one time, and believe me, I had offers. Most of the time it was hoors trying to get out of being arrested, but you get my drift.'

She sat silently for a bit. 'My ex was a womaniser. He hid it very well, until he tried to sleep with a woman he didn't realise was a friend of mine. She delayed telling me, but in the end she couldn't keep it a secret anymore. It was eating her up. Jack and I divorced two years ago.'

'I've no time for people like that. Sorry.'

'No need to apologise. It's a nice trait in a man.'

As they drove into Edinburgh, Bracken thought about this woman sitting in the car with him. She was from Inverness but had worked in Edinburgh before, as she knew Bob Long. He was sure he'd seen her before. Not just in passing but in some capacity. He couldn't put his finger on it.

They chitchatted about life, about staying at the

guest house, about how she'd beaten his dad at poker but thought he was a hustler.

'He's harmless but he does like a wee game of poker or two. You're right to watch him.'

'I like him.'

'Good. You can take him home with you when you get the house sorted.' He smiled at her.

'The way my life's going, he'd be the only man who'd want to come home with me.'

'You're selling yourself short there, ma'am.'

'I give off a vibe of being a mean old baddie.'

'Not to me, you don't.' He stopped himself there, in case she thought he was flirting with her.

They went inside, where the team were waiting. Sullivan and Izzie were back from the mortuary.

'How did it go?' Bracken asked them. Kara went upstairs to her office.

'Pam Green found something stuffed in Maxine's throat,' said Sullivan. 'It was a little piece of paper with a date printed on it. From a newspaper.'

'It's on its way to forensics, yes?'

'It is, but I took a photo of it so we could have a look. I had it blown up and put the photo on the whiteboard.'

Bracken read it. 'What happened on that day?' he asked no one in particular. 'December second, twenty-seventeen.' He turned to look at Sullivan. 'Any ideas?'

'Nothing that jumps out. I'm doing searches of the newspapers online,' Izzie said.

Angie Paton walked up to Bracken. 'Can I have a word for a minute, sir?'

'Sure. What's up?' They walked over to a quiet corner of the room.

'My wife and I are having a party on Hogmanay. Sort of a New Year's party and housewarming combined. I'd like to invite you along. I know it's short notice and I know you probably have a party already lined up, but you're welcome to come.'

'Thanks for that. I'm not sure what's happening yet. My dad's in town for a week and I'm hoping he won't need putting to bed blootered.'

'I'll text you my new address later, just in case you can make it. Meantime, Edwin Hawk is waiting in one of the interview rooms.'

'Thanks, Angie.'

He walked over to Sullivan. 'Let's go and talk to Hawk.'

Before they left the incident room, Bracken's phone rang. He answered it. It was Cameron Robb with the information he wanted. He thanked him and hung up.

They went down a corridor just as Kara was walking down the stairs. 'There's an empty office next to yours in the incident room, isn't there?' she asked him.

'Yes, there is.'

'Good. I want to move in there. All this up and down the stairs, it's nonsense. I'd rather be closer to the team. I'll be along in the observation room shortly.'

'Yes, ma'am.'

'Didn't you say you struggled with the stairs too?' Sullivan said to Bracken as they walked away.

'No, I didn't, cheeky bastard. I'm as fit as the rest of them in here.'

'Huh. I thought I heard your smart watch squealing and shouting, calling for help. Dialling treble-nine. Maybe it meant there was a fire nearby.'

'You'll be fired in a minute. Get your arse in that room.'

They went in, and the uniform who was cutting off Hawk's only means of escape left.

'Mr Hawk, we meet again,' Bracken said as they sat down at the table opposite the doctor. Writer.

Possible serial killer.

TWENTY-TWO

'I wish it was under better circumstances, but I have to admit, I can glean some information for my research with this request to come into the station.' Hawk gave a cocky smile and tapped his fingers on the table top. 'What am I supposed to have done now?'

Bracken didn't feel like doing the dance today. 'Stella Graham is dead.'

Hawk's mouth moved up and down like a goldfish out of its bowl. 'Dead. What do you mean, dead?'

'It's self-explanatory,' Sullivan said.

'She can't be. I only saw her last...' Hawk's voice trailed off. 'Oh, crap.'

'What's wrong?' Bracken said.

'She sent me a text last night. After we had an early dinner, she caught the train home to Kirkcaldy.'

'What time was that?'

'She got the eight-fifteen. It would have got her there for around nine o'clock. It was just after nine that I got the text from her.' Hawk took his phone out and showed the screen to the two detectives.

Hawk, please come! I don't want to go home. I thought about it on the train and I want to be with you now. I want to get my stuff from the house, but I don't want to go in alone. I'll wait at the station for you. Love you. Xxx

'Let me guess,' Bracken said, 'you hopped into your car and drove over.'

'I did. I hired a car for the duration of my stay, but I hadn't used it much. Driving in Edinburgh is even worse than driving in Manhattan. But it was in the hotel's underground car park if I needed it.'

'What happened when you got there?' Sullivan asked. 'You had an argument and killed her?'

'Jesus, no, nothing like that. I loved Stella. She was going to be my wife. I would have given her a far better life than that asshole she lived with.'

'Oh, I don't know,' Bracken said. 'I was at their house this morning and it's a nice place they have.'

'Yes, she told me about her house. But a house doesn't make a home. Tom works on the oil rigs and he's a mean drunk.'

Bracken thought back to the way Stella's husband had answered the door and he could believe that.

Hawk carried on. 'She was going to wait until he went back to the rigs, then she was going to leave him. Then, as we told you yesterday, she would come over to the States on a fiancée visa, and then we would get married. They just stayed in the house in different rooms.'

Bracken sat back in his seat. 'Something doesn't quite click into place. First of all, a fiancée visa for America means you would have ninety days to get married to Stella, but it would have taken longer than that for Stella's divorce to come through.'

'They weren't married officially. Believe it or not, they were already divorced. You can check. They got divorced a few years back and went their own ways. Then he came back into her life. He promised her he'd stopped drinking. He'd bought the house; Stella's name wasn't on the deeds, but she moved in. Things were good for a year, she said, then the drinking started in earnest again. And things went back to the way they were. He started hitting her.'

'We *are* going to check all of this.'

'Please do! And while you're at it, look into her husband again!'

'He seems to think they're still married,' Bracken said.

'They were almost like husband and wife. Except for the divorced part. He doesn't seem to think there's anything wrong. She's scared of him and wants to leave.' Hawk lowered his head. 'Wanted.'

'He has an alibi,' said Bracken. 'Before I came in here, a colleague from Fife called me. He checked out Tom Graham's alibi and several people confirmed he was in a pub at the time Stella was murdered. It wasn't him. That just leaves you. Tell us what happened when you got there.'

'I got to the station parking lot, sorry, car park, and her car was there. A Beetle. I parked next to it, since the car park was practically empty. There was nobody about. No sign of Stella. I texted her. Read it for yourself.'

Bracken did.

I'm here, honey. Where are you?

No reply. Five minutes passed.

Can you talk? Are you at the house? Please tell me you didn't go there alone? If you want me to come along, I will. I just want to know you're safe.

No reply.

Bracken showed the messages to Sullivan.

'This was just before ten p.m.,' Bracken said.

'I know. By the time I got the car out of the hotel and drove across, it was just before ten. I'm not the fastest driver on the wrong side of the road.' Hawk's breathing was faster now, like he was getting even more agitated.

'We believe Stella was killed sometime after ten p.m. We believe her killer had taken her by then.'

'I didn't touch her! I love her!' Hawk started moving forward in his chair but then slumped back, tears running down his face. 'Loved. No, that's wrong. I still love her. I don't want anybody else. I didn't lay a finger on her. I would never harm her.'

'What was Stella's day job when she wasn't helping you with your research?' Bracken asked, wanting to see if Hawk's answer would be the same as Tom Graham's.

'She was a psychiatric nurse. At the Royal Edinburgh.'

'Where you worked when you lived here?'

'Yes. It's how we met.'

They were silent for a moment before Bracken spoke again. 'You know, I've charged men with less evidence.'

'Are you going to charge me? Even though I'm innocent?'

'Innocent until proven guilty.' Bracken sat forward with his fingers on the table again. 'You see where I'm having a problem: this timing doesn't fit. You just said you don't drive quickly here because we drive on the wrong side of the road, but you lived here for three years, give or take. Didn't you drive back then?'

Bracken already knew the answer, which was contained in the file in front of him.

'Yes. I did have a car.'

'What kind of car did you drive?' Again, he unconsciously tapped the buff folder.

'It was a Beetle.'

'The same Beetle that Stella now drives?'

Hawk locked eyes with him before answering. 'Yes. I sold it to her. For next to nothing, but she wanted to give me a hundred pounds for it so she could look Tom in the eyes and say genuinely that she'd bought it from a colleague.'

Bracken looked at Sullivan. 'How long would you say the drive to Kirkcaldy would take on a Sunday evening when the traffic is light?'

Sullivan shrugged. 'Twenty, twenty-five minutes. No more.'

'Interesting. You hear that, Hawk? Twenty or twenty-five minutes. Now, I know it took closer to forty minutes for me to drive over there today because of all the Formula One wannabes taking up road space, but on a Sunday evening? The church crowd are tucked up in bed, the drunks are still in the pubs and the teenage hooligans aren't racing on the motorway. And we know perfectly well you can drive just fine on these roads. You have a British driving licence after all. So let's say you read the text and the adrenaline is pumping. Now you've got a case of the Jackie Stewart's, booting it up the motorway.'

'It wasn't like that.'

'Stella gets to the station after nine, sends you a text. So you get to the car, get on the road, take twenty minutes for the actual drive…Let's give you the benefit of the doubt and say you get there at nine forty-five. That still gives you fifteen minutes to abduct Stella and take her to the crime scene, where you kill her. It's a five-minute drive. Let's say you get there sometime after ten. You have time to do what it is you do and then set the fire. The call came in at ten thirty-one, to be precise. It's isolated, so you piss off in your car again and make it back to Edinburgh before…'

Bracken caught himself.

'Before what?'

'Is that how it went, more or less?' he answered, ignoring Hawk's question.

'No, it didn't go like that at all.'

'Then tell us how it did go. Get it off your chest. You'll feel better if you tell us why you killed her.'

'I didn't kill her. I keep telling you that.'

Sullivan sat forward. 'You admitted you were there. Beside her car. You sent her a text to keep up the pretence that you couldn't find her.'

Bracken opened the file, finally. 'You worked at the Royal Edinburgh. Stella also worked there, as a psychiatric nurse. Know who else worked there?'

Hawk sat staring at him.

'It was a rhetorical question. Maxine Graham. She was a social worker. The three of you worked hand in hand. Isn't that right?'

'Yes.'

'Now we have two female victims you worked with. Both killed in the space of two nights. Which leads me to ask: where's Tracey Pitman? You know, the woman who's fallen in love with you? The woman who is such a burden to you. Did you kill her as well? You might as well get it off your chest, Hawk. In for a penny and all that. Where is she?'

'I didn't kill her, I didn't kill Maxine and I most certainly didn't kill Stella!' Hawk slammed a fist on the table.

'How can we be sure?'

Hawk sat back, his face flushed, but he remained silent.

'You made a phone call when you got here. Did you call a lawyer?'

Hawk sat silently, then a few seconds later the door opened.

'No, he called me,' Stuart McDonald said. The Scottish justice minster closed the door behind him and sat next to Hawk.

'We're going to have to tell them,' he said.

TWENTY-THREE

Bracken and McDonald looked at each other over the table.

'Once again, DCI Bracken, I am immensely grateful that you saved my son's life. However, I can't stand by and watch an innocent man go down for murder.'

'How do you know he's innocent?'

McDonald looked between him and Hawk. 'I was with him last night.'

Bracken couldn't contain his surprise. 'That could be construed as a confession,' he said.

'But it's not. I can vouch for Hawk here. I went to Fife with him. He called me in a panic. He knew something was wrong with Stella, and I said I would drive through with him. I did the driving. You're right, it only takes twenty minutes in a Jag.'

'Didn't you have a Mercedes? I seem to remember one sitting in your driveway.'

'I traded it in. I couldn't even look at it after...well, you know.'

'Understandable.'

'Anyway, I picked Hawk up at the hotel. The doorman will confirm that. We drove quickly through to Kirkcaldy, and Stella's Beetle was indeed at the station. We drove along to her house, but there were no lights on. That doesn't mean much, but when you put the jigsaw pieces together, you have two men looking for her and an ex-husband who was in the pub, which leaves only one conclusion.'

Bracken nodded. 'She was taken by somebody else.'

'Correct.'

'I would hazard a guess that she knew her abductor,' Sullivan said. 'It stands to reason. There would've been other people around at the station – not many at that time, but still witnesses who'd have seen him. He was confident enough to take her from the station because she went with him willingly.'

'That's a good point,' McDonald said. 'Who would she have got into a car with?'

'Tracey Pitman. Maybe she pretended to want to talk,' Sullivan said.

'No,' Hawk replied. 'Stella wouldn't get in the car with Tracey. I told her to stay away from Tracey.'

'My former DI will be working with Kirkcaldy CID to see if they can find some CCTV cameras near the station. See if we can see a car leaving or close to it around the time the train pulled in,' Bracken said.

There was silence for a moment, broken by McDonald. 'You might well be wondering how Hawk came to call me.'

More silence. *Oh, do fucking enlighten us,* Bracken thought.

'Let me explain. I knew Hawk from when he worked in the Royal Edinburgh. So while he was here on his book tour, I asked him to do an independent evaluation of Ailsa Connolly, since he isn't her doctor anymore.'

'Ailsa?' Bracken said. A psychologist who had killed six men.

'Yes. We both believe, Hawk and I, that Ailsa killed those men while she was under great mental distress and not of sound mind. We believe that she is of sound mind now, and he's going to assess her. The sticking point until now was that people thought she'd killed children as well. Now that we know she didn't and the real killer of those kids is being held in Carstairs until his trial, we can proceed with a view to having Ailsa released. Under supervision at first, but she'll be able to carry on with her studies, leading to her becoming a fully-fledged Church of Scotland minister.'

Hawk nodded. 'Sorry, I couldn't tell you because this has to be kept in the strictest confidence. I will give her a fair and unbiased appraisal. I know her, since she was one of my patients for a couple of years before I left.'

Bracken had hated Ailsa Connolly but now understood her better.

'You know she tried to kill me too?' he asked Hawk.

'That was always up for debate. You suspected she was going to poison you and then kill you, but there was never any definitive proof.'

Bracken knew that was true, but he was the one who'd been there that night in her flat.

'When is this assessment happening?' Bracken asked Hawk.

'Tomorrow. Midday. You can come along and observe. She likes you.'

'I'll be there.'

McDonald stood up and motioned for Hawk to do the same. 'I can safely say that neither of us is on your suspect list now, Bracken?'

Bracken took a deep breath before answering. The chances that this writer and the justice minster had gone through to Fife and burned a woman to death were slim to none. He stood up.

'You're free to go, Mr Hawk. Thank you for helping us with our enquiries.'

Hawk stood up. 'No hard feelings, Sean.' He'd started to leave the room with McDonald when Bracken stopped him.

'If we think Tracey was capable of killing Maxine and Stella because they both worked at the hospital, then you could be a target too.'

'I know. I had thought of that. Unless she was getting rid of what she saw as competition. Even though Maxine and I only ever had a working relationship, Tracey might not have looked at it that way.'

'Have you any idea where she might be hiding out?'

'She was supposed to have gone to live with her father, and she did, I believe. If she's not there, then I don't know where she is. Sorry.'

Both men walked out, leaving Bracken and Sullivan alone in the room.

'Square one, eh?' Bracken said. 'She's not with her father. We checked.'

'Aye, back to the drawing board, boss.'

They went back to the incident room, where Kara was waiting. 'We need to get everybody looking for this Tracey Pitman.'

'To be honest, I think we're barking up the wrong tree,' said Bracken.

'Really? How so? You told Hawk he might be a target too,' Sullivan said.

'That's if Tracey is indeed the killer. I'm not a hundred per cent certain she is. She was put in the Royal Edinburgh because she was mentally unstable and set fire to a barn. Hawk worked with her and he deemed her fit to go back into society,' Bracken said.

'And look at her now – she wants him for herself. Do you think he made a mistake?'

'My feeling is she's just in love with him. Would she kill for him? Only he would know that because he was her doctor. It's a tricky one. But this killer is so organised. Tracey seems a bit unstable, incapable of such organisation.'

'She's the only suspect we have just now,' Kara said. 'The team are working their way through the names of the people who were at the signing on Saturday night, and they're all older people who belong to golf clubs and Rotary clubs, and not one of them has a criminal record. We're going to go through their alibis as well, like where they went after the talk, but so far most of them have said they went home.'

'That just leaves the Tracey Pitman angle and I think that's walking down the wrong road,' Bracken said.

'We could be looking at a complete stranger,' Kara said.

'One thing I'd like to say: please don't let my dad get under your skin. He means well.'

She smiled at him. 'I like him a lot. He reminds me of my own dad, who isn't here anymore. Besides, I'm going to take him to the cleaners.'

'Remember what I said to him about not gambling with my inheritance.'

'Oh, I think he's way beyond that. But one more thing: I knew about tomorrow, obviously, and I'll be there too. It's been a long time.'

She turned and walked away, leaving Bracken wondering what she meant.

TWENTY-FOUR

'You look like somebody's stolen your ball,' Natalie Hogan said as Bracken entered the guest house.

He wondered where Natalie would have been right now if she hadn't been arrested. Would she still have been married to Stuart McDonald?

'A young woman was burnt to death after being tied to a metal chair and we're trying to catch her killer.'

'Oh, God, I'm sorry. I didn't mean to sound flippant.'

He gave her a weak smile. 'It's fine, don't worry about it. This case has got my head spinning. Just when we think we've got a breakthrough, it gets turned on its head.'

'If you ever want to sit and talk about it, I'm free most nights.'

'You've got wee Rory to look after.'

'For the time being. When his father gets settled, he'll be taking him back. He has full custody, remember?'

'I'm sure you can both work it out.'

She put a hand on his arm. 'I'll never be able to repay you for saving Rory's life.'

'You don't have to.'

'Unless...'

Oh Christ, please don't ask me up to your room. He waited for her to carry on.

'What I was going to say is, if you don't want to talk to me about your case, maybe I could run my eyes over the details. I mean, it doesn't have to be anything confidential, but me and Bob often sit and watch true crime shows and try to guess who the killer is. It would be another two sets of eyes on it.'

'Sure. I don't have any paperwork with me, but after dinner I'll go over it with you both.'

'Good. See you in the living room.' She smiled and walked away upstairs.

Bob Long came through from the back. 'Steak and kidney pie for dinner,' he said, throwing a dish towel over one shoulder.

'Sounds good. But listen, I want to run something past you.'

'As long as it's not your bloody baton again,' he replied, making a face.

'I've got it firmly in my pocket.'

'We'll have none of that talk in here, pal.' He laughed.

Bracken groaned. 'Your bloody dad jokes don't get much better, do they?'

'Oh, I've got plenty, son.'

Years before he got divorced, Bracken and his wife would make up a foursome with Bob and Mary, since Bob was a DI, the same as Bracken. It had been Fife who had promoted Bracken to DCI.

Bob and Mary hadn't been blessed with children and now he had turned fifty that ship had sailed for Bob. He also had a broken back, which had disabled him out of the force.

'Anyway, I was thinking about Kara earlier,' said Bracken.

'Jesus, you're skating on thin ice there, pal. Best to leave romance out of the workplace.'

'Will you shut your hole for a minute?'

'You play with fire, you get burnt.'

'I'm not playing with fire. I just want to ask you a question.'

'I'm all ears.'

'Mouth more like it, but that's another story.'

'Christ, I miss our slagging each other off, Sean.'

'I have to admit, we had some good laughs. But seriously, pal, I want to ask you about when you worked with Kara.'

Bob looked around like a clown in a silent movie. 'Go ahead.'

'When you said you worked with her a while back, in what capacity was that?'

'She was on the Ailsa Connolly task force.'

Bracken nodded. That was it. 'Thanks, Bob. I thought I recognised her face from somewhere. And we're going to see Ailsa tomorrow.'

'Oh, really?'

Just a week ago, Bob would have shoved cocktail sticks under Ailsa's fingernails, but after what had happened to them all the week before, he'd come to see her in a different light. That and the fact she hadn't killed the kids he thought she had.

'I can't talk about it, but all will be revealed in good time.'

'Aye, well.' Bob looked at Bracken for a moment, all joviality gone. He turned on his heel and went back through to his private quarters.

Bracken knew it would take a while for his friend to fully come to terms with Ailsa Connolly trying to get released again.

They'd have to deal with that when it happened.

TWENTY-FIVE

Edwin Hawk and Stuart McDonald sat in the bar of the hotel.

'Just as well you were with me, Stu, or I'd be toast.'

'I'm not going to have you arrested and charged for something you didn't do. Trust me, I've seen a lot of lowlifes walk free and they were guilty. We all knew it, they knew it, but the bloody evidence wasn't there. You're innocent, and by God you're not going to do time for somebody else's crime.'

'Thanks, buddy. I appreciate it. Another single malt?'

'Well, since you're talking like that, why not?'

Hawk got up and went to the bar. He was ordering the drinks when he saw an older man walk in, clunking his walking stick on the stone floor.

'Hey, pal!' he said, noting the carrier bag in the old man's hand.

'Hello again, Hawk. I have the books for you to sign, just like you said you would,' Donald Masterson said.

Hawk was at the point where the amount of alcohol consumed was just about to tip the scales from sobriety into inebriated, and his welcome was overenthusiastic.

'Donald, what you having? My good buddy Stuart is over there and we're getting wired into the malts. You having one?'

'Oh, well, that's very kind. Maybe just a little one.'

'Make 'em doubles, barkeep, and put them on my slate.'

'With a little bit of water for me, thanks,' Masterson said.

'You heard the man. Touch of the old water.' Hawk put an arm around Masterson, who made a face like Hawk had just suggested he iron his underpants while he was still wearing them.

'Right, my little friend, take a hold of one of these Scottish crystals and we'll head on over to my pal,' Hawk said, taking hold of the carrier bag.

'That's very kind, but I can't stay long.'

'Stay as long as you want.'

Hawk introduced McDonald, and Masterson seemed overawed by the powerful man.

'As much as I'd like to stay and have a few more, this is my one for the road, Hawk,' McDonald said. 'We have a busy day ahead of us tomorrow.'

Masterson sipped his whisky and Hawk took out some of the books that Masterson had brought along. 'I put the word out, and my friends at the museum and on the council would like a signed copy.'

'I appreciate the word-of-mouth recommendations, Donald, my friend. You're a star.'

'Och, away with you. It's always a pleasure talking about your books.'

Hawk took the proffered pen, signed a few books and gave them back to Masterson.

'I appreciate it, Hawk. My friends will be over the moon.' Masterson smiled, then took a sip of the whisky.

'Anytime, my friend. I'm having a wee get-together with some friends on Hogmanay. Get yourself along here. Unless you have other plans?'

'I'm going to a party with my girlfriend, but thanks anyway.'

'Girlfriend, eh? You're a dark horse. What's her name?'

Masterson looked flustered for a moment. 'Nobody you would know. Anyway, got to go. Thanks a bunch for signing the books.' He stood up and threw the whisky down his throat and walked out without saying another word.

'Donald Masterson with a girlfriend? Who would have thought it?' Hawk said.

'Right, I'm going to go as well,' said McDonald. 'We need a clear head for tomorrow. I'm counting on you for this one, Hawk.'

'I guess I should stop it there. But before we go.' Hawk raised his glass. 'To Stella.'

'To Stella.'

They finished their whiskies and put the glasses down. They shook hands.

'Tomorrow. Twelve o'clock.'

'You made it later in the morning so I could sober up, didn't you?' Hawk said, smiling.

'I know you too well. Take care. See you at the hospital.'

TWENTY-SIX

The house phone rang and Bob Long answered it, about to tell some pond-life telemarketer what he would do to him if they ever met up face to face, but it wasn't a telemarketer or anybody else trying to sell things.

It was Kara Page's ex-husband.

'I'll go and get her for you.'

He carried the phone through from his living room and put the receiver on the small hallway table out in the guests' section. He moved up the stairs as fast as a man with a broken back can move and knocked on her door.

'Your ex is on the house phone for you,' he said when she answered.

'Thanks, Bob.'

'Nae bother.' He scooted down the stairs and went

back into his private quarters.

Kara picked up the receiver. 'Tony, how did you know I was staying here? And why can't you call my mobile number?'

'I thought this would be more private,' said a thick, obviously disguised voice.

'Who is this?' She took her mobile phone out, opened the camera, slid along to video and started recording.

'Never mind who I am. You shouldn't have come back here, Kara. I thought the little redecorating would have made you go back north, but you're not easily persuaded. But maybe you'll be persuaded when you see Tony's lifeless corpse.'

'What the hell are you talking about?' She felt a mixture of tough copper and panicking ex-wife. 'Why are you doing this?'

'You sound like a young girl on a first date who's found out what her boyfriend really wants and is about to be taken by force.'

'Why don't you come and see me? We can talk this through.'

Maniacal laughter on the other end. 'We *are* going to talk this through. Tonight. Or else Tony dies. You and me can talk and then your ex lives. You know where to meet me, Kara. Come alone. I'll be watching from a distance. When I'm sure you haven't been stupid and brought somebody, I'll approach. Then you'll find out why I want to speak to you up close and personal.'

'I'll be there.'

'Twenty minutes. Alone, bitch.'

The line went dead and she cut the call on Bob's phone. Then she put her head against the wall.

'You okay?'

She gasped and jumped back, creating a fist, her middle knuckle extended.

'Easy, Kara, it's just me,' Bob Long said, coming back for his phone. 'I wasn't earwigging, but I saw the line was clear again.'

'Christ, I thought it was him.'

'Who?'

'The man who just called. He's going to kill my ex-husband. I only have twenty minutes.'

'To do what?' he asked, stepping closer.

'He wants me alone, Bob. I have to go.' She picked up her phone and stopped the recording. She rewound part of it to let him hear.

'I'll be watching from a distance. When I'm sure you haven't been stupid and brought somebody, I'll approach. Then you'll find out why I want to speak to you up close and personal.'

It sounded like a robot. 'He's using a voice changer. Where does he want you to go?'

'My house. That's the only place I can get to in twenty minutes from here. Just.'

'I'm coming with you.'

'No! Didn't you hear what he said? He's going to kill Tony.'

'Have you tried calling him?' Bob asked.

'I don't have his number. There's no reason to call him anymore, but I don't want to be the cause of his death.'

He put his hands on her shoulders. 'You're not thinking like a copper now. You're thinking like a victim. It happens, don't worry. It's a normal reaction. We, as detectives, can cut through the emotions when we're dealing with victims, but right now you're a victim of this guy. I'm not letting you go alone.'

'You have to. He's going to kill Tony. I can't let that happen. Promise me you won't come!'

Bob was starting to get flustered. 'I promise!'

'If I don't call you in an hour, bring the cavalry.' She grabbed her car keys and left the house.

Ed Bracken came out of the living room. 'That was a smashing dinner, Bob,' he said. 'Your Mary can certainly cook.'

'Thanks, pal,' Bob said, but he was preoccupied.

'I wasn't listening, but I'm not deaf either. I was the only one in there, so nobody else heard, but I heard everything. I might not have been a copper like my son or you, but I've watched enough TV shows to know she's walking into a trap. Come alone. Don't tell anybody. He's going to harm her, you know that?'

'I do, Ed, but she made me promise.'

'I know she did. And you can keep that promise and still help her.'

'How do I do that?'

Ed held up a finger before bringing his mobile phone out and dialling a number. A few seconds after he spoke, they heard a door upstairs opening and closing.

'Lazy old sod,' Bracken said, coming down the stairs. 'I'm getting ready to go out.'

'I know you are. And less of your bloody lip. Kara got a wonky phone call from some arsehole and made Bob here promise he wouldn't go. She's in danger.'

Bracken looked serious. 'Where did she go?'

'Her house in Ratho,' Bob answered. 'He said he's got her ex-husband, Tony, and he's going to kill him if she doesn't go and get him.'

'Did she try to call Tony?'

'She doesn't have his number.'

'Christ, first her house was vandalised and now this,' Ed said.

'She's walking into a trap. The damage was just to get her attention, to make sure she took him seriously,' Bracken said.

Bob shook his head. 'I don't know who this is, but she can't go there alone.'

'She's not going alone.' Bracken looked at his father. 'Before you ask, no, you can't come along for the ride.'

'I'm going. I don't care that I promised her,' Bob said.

'Me too. Another pair of eyes,' Ed replied.

'I said no. I'm not putting either of you in danger.'

'If you don't bring us along, Bob will just drive me and himself up there.'

'What's wrong with your heid? I am not putting you in danger.'

Ed smiled and walked up to his son. 'You might be bigger, and louder, than me, but I am your father. You'll do as you're bloody well told.'

'Sean, he only gave her twenty minutes.'

'Christ. Bob, take your car, put your hazards on, follow me, then back off when we get near. I'll go in with my lights off. Any sign of danger, you boot it the hell out of there. Understand?'

'Aye.' Bob grinned. 'I'll get my car keys.' He turned and moved back to the private quarters.

'Good boy,' Ed said.

'I'm going to train Max to bite your arse,' Bracken said, turning back to the stairs to go and get his jacket.

TWENTY-SEVEN

Kara drove quickly along Glasgow Road, the blue flashers behind the grille of her 5 Series parting the traffic, helped by the siren. Across the Gogar Roundabout and left into Gogar Station Road, past the Royal Bank of Scotland HQ. The road had been gritted, but light snow was falling; her car had all-wheel drive and handled the conditions with aplomb. She reduced her speed as a couple of cars came from the opposite direction.

She turned right and turned off the siren and flashers. She looked at the dashboard clock; it had taken her a little over ten minutes, so she had time to slow the car down on the road, which was starting to get a little slicker. The gritter truck had left snow piled up at the side of the road.

Her house was on the left at the intersection with

Hermiston House Road. She slowed to a walking pace and turned the headlights off, leaving the sidelights on, and turned into her driveway. It was a large, detached house and that had appealed when she'd bought, it a few years ago. She looked over to the detached garage where a woman had been killed a week or so ago.

She put the lights out and darkness gripped the house and the gardens, but there was still plenty of snow on the ground, making it lighter than normal. What in the name of God had ever possessed her to buy a house in the wilderness? Peace and quiet was one thing, but isolation was another. It was almost like living off-grid being out here.

Her car was white and didn't stick out too much, so she was thankful for that. She eased the door open, making sure her extendable baton was in her pocket. Since she had never been one for high heels, she still had her work boots on.

She looked around her, not keeping her gaze focused on one point for too long. She didn't need her pocket torch, but she held on to it anyway. She locked the car before walking towards the front door, always moving her head. As she got closer, she saw a faint light coming through the crack in the curtains in the living room.

The front door was ajar.

She gently nudged it open, the cold air rushing in

with her. The house was freezing and she was shivering, the cold digging into her bones.

She shone the torch around. She thought she remembered where all the creaky floorboards were, but memory didn't serve her well. She stood on one and it yelled like it was in pain.

The living room was on the right, and she went in through the open doorway to where the light was flickering. As she went in, she saw the back of her ex-husband's head. He was sitting tied to a chair further into the room.

She quickly looked around, flashing the light into every dark corner, but nobody else was there.

She approached Tony, scared to speak up in case he couldn't hear her. In case he was dead.

'Hello, Kara,' the voice said from the doorway.

She spun round, pointing the torchlight at the masked face. Then she smelled it. Too late.

He threw the petrol bomb into the room and the petrol he'd poured meticulously around the room caught fire.

She was trapped.

And she was going to die.

TWENTY-EIGHT

Bracken put his lights out as he approached Hermiston House Road. He'd come down that road a week earlier and remembered his life flashing before his eyes as his car tried to make an arse of him.

'Aye, you know fucking better now, wee bastard,' he told it. His head was still reeling from Bob telling him that Kara owned the house where one of the victims from his previous case had been found.

How long had Bob known?

He looked in his rear-view mirror and was glad to see Bob had put his hazards off now and was driving only with his sidelights on. Bracken stopped his car, rolled the window down and pointed a finger over the roof; *park here*, he was telling them.

And his bloody dad coming along. What in the name of Christ was he thinking? He knew Bob Long had an excuse, but his old man? Ed had never been a copper. He'd been an accounts manager for BT. Crunching numbers all day.

He fired the car up to Kara's house then jumped on the brakes. Shoved the car into reverse, moved back at high speed and skidded to a stop near where Bob had parked his car. His friend was out of the driver's seat, encumbered by his broken back, and even Ed was out of the car.

'What's wrong, Sean?' Bob shouted, his polis instincts kicking in.

'The fucking house is on fire! Call the fire brigade! And stay here!'

Bracken ran forward to Kara's house and saw her BMW parked out front. The flames had caught the curtains in the living room and from what he could see it was well alight.

The front door was open and he ran inside without any thought for his own safety. Just like the night he had done the same thing and saved Bob Long's life.

Smoke was belching out everywhere and he put an arm over his mouth.

'Kara! Kara! Where are you?' he shouted at the top of his voice, keeping his head ducked down, trying to get lower, where the fresher air was.

He heard a scream come from the living room. The door was open and he thought he saw movement. He caught a glimpse of Kara. He pulled his coat up over his head and held it with one hand as he raced through the flames in the doorway.

He saw her struggling with a curtain in the middle of the room, trying to beat out the flames in a futile attempt to extinguish the fire. She dropped to her knees, coughing. He ran through the immense heat, knowing he only had seconds to get to her.

He grabbed her by the collar of her coat, lifted her up, threw her over his shoulder and ran full tilt through the flames again, rushing back outside, where he roughly tossed her down onto the snow on the front lawn.

She was coughing, which was a good sign. Her eyes were closed, and then suddenly they snapped wide open, and he saw her tense as she coughed and knew her fist was about to connect with his face.

He grabbed her arm and put his face closer to hers. 'Kara! It's me, Sean! You're safe now. You're safe. I've got you.'

There was smoke coming off her long coat.

'Sean? What are you doing here?'

'Jesus, coming up here alone. You should have told me.'

Then she sat up quickly. 'Tony! He's in there!'

'Did you see where he was?'

'In the living room, tied to a chair. There was a hood over his head.'

Bracken looked at the flames roaring through the house and knew there was no chance of a rescue. His dad and Bob Long came into the driveway.

'Kara!' Bob shouted. 'Are you okay?'

She looked at the two men. 'You promised you wouldn't come.'

Bob and Ed pointed a finger at Bracken. 'He made us,' Ed said.

'The fire brigade are on their way, but some bastard came booting out of a wee lane off that side road,' Bob said.

'What are the chances you got his licence number?'

'About the same as Posh Spice leaving David for you. His lights were out, but I saw it was one of those short Land Rovers the farmers use. Looked dark green. He went tearing down the road, then just as he turned the corner, he put his lights on. I already called it in, so they can look for it, but God knows where he'll go now.'

'Good job. Now, give me a hand to get Kara on her feet.' Bracken looked at his boss. 'Where're your car keys?'

She fished them out of her pocket. Bracken took them and handed them to his dad.

'Move her car out of the way. If you can still remember how to drive.'

'Listen, son, I was driving before you were even a twinkle in my eye.'

'Christ, that conjures up all sorts of images. But go and move it now before the fire brigade get here.'

Ed rushed towards the car while Bracken and Bob held on to Kara, guiding her out of the driveway. She stopped a few times, attempting to dislodge one of her lungs, but they got her to the main road before Stirling Moss backed the car out like a racing driver, which Bracken thought was more luck than skill.

The old man reversed and parked beside Bob's and Bracken's cars, blocking the driveway of the other house. A man came storming along the drive from the side of the house.

'Here! What's the meaning of this?'

'Will you tell him to fuck off or will I?' Ed asked.

'Just rein it in a wee bit,' Bracken said. Then to the neighbour: 'Police. There's a fire in the house across the way.'

'I don't care what the hell is going on. You can't block my driveway.'

Sensing that his son was about to say something, Ed stepped forward.

'My name's Ed Bracken. Now, you can be a dick

about this, and when we're gone, we'll do so much background research on you, if you've got so much as an outstanding parking ticket, we'll have this place stripped apart, just before we strip your life apart. You'd better be squeaky clean. Or, you can be a good citizen and have a look at the video your security camera caught and see if it picked up the licence number on the car that just came out of that wee lane back there. Choice is yours. You might even be turned into a hero.'

The man looked at Bracken. 'I'll go and have a look. Give me five minutes.' He turned on the snow-covered driveway and marched back inside.

'Good lad,' Ed said to his back.

'Christ Almighty. In front of my superintendent. What are you like?'

'He's just helping, Sean,' Kara said between coughs. 'I'd have him on my team any day.'

'Hear that?' Ed said. 'Kara would have me on her team any day.'

'She's hallucinating from the smoke inhalation.'

'Whatever helps you sleep at night.'

'Right now, it's some pills and a bottle of vodka.'

They heard the sirens in the distance. Fire engines, police cars, ambulance. Maybe if they were lucky, a coastguard helicopter.

Kara looked at Bracken. 'Thank you for coming.

All of you.' She turned her attention to Bob. 'Just as well you don't obey my bloody orders.'

He smiled at her. 'That's what being a retired copper gets you: no more bosses to listen to.'

'Except Mary,' Bracken said.

'That's it, spoil the illusion.'

Kara looked at Bob and Ed. 'You two had better get away before too many questions are asked. As far as I'm concerned, you were never here.'

Bob tapped Ed on the arm and they got into Bob's car and left.

Kara had a coughing fit as the first ambulance arrived, just in front of the fire engine.

TWENTY-NINE

Bracken was tired, but he still got up early. There was no sign of his dad when he went down for a coffee, but Chaz was having breakfast in the dining room, sitting chatting with Bob.

Bracken looked puzzled.

Chaz smiled at him. 'Bob called me last night and told me what happened. I sent you a text asking if you needed me for anything, but you were busy.'

'Yeah, I got caught up in things. You two got home in one piece, I see,' he said to Bob.

'Me and Ed never left the house last night, son. You must be thinking of somebody else.'

'Okay, did Batman and Robin get back in one piece?'

'You want some toast or a cooked breakfast?' Bob asked, ignoring the question.

'I can make the toast, thanks. I really need a coffee.'

'I'll leave you both to it.'

'Don't make it sound like I'll be leaping on her,' Bracken said.

'I'll fight him off, Bob, don't worry.' Chaz smiled at Bob as he left. After what they had gone through just a week earlier, Bob and Chaz had bonded.

'I can barely find the energy to butter my toast. If I can put it in the toaster in the first place.' Bracken finally managed it and poured a coffee, then stood beside Chaz. 'Is anybody sitting there?'

The dining room was empty and a small lamp barely lit the room in the darkness.

'Well, I'm waiting for a man who's tall, handsome, intelligent, funny...'

'Please. You'll have me blushing in a minute.'

'But he won't be coming, so you may as well sit down.'

'I was waiting for that bloody punchline. You need new material, Chaz Cullen.'

He sat down opposite her and she put a hand on his. 'Seriously, I was worried when Bob called. He suggested I come over and have breakfast with you.'

'It's just gone six-thirty. You must be...' *Keen*, he was going to say, but he hesitated. 'Energetic,' he said instead.

'Ready, willing and able,' she said, taking her hand back.

'I'll bear that in mind if I want to train for a marathon.'

'Seriously, I heard what happened to Kara. I hope she's going to be okay.'

'Just a little smoke inhalation. They kept her in overnight for observation, but she's lucky. She wasn't in that room for long.'

'She would have died if it wasn't for you. You saved her life.'

'Bob tell you that, did he?'

'Yes, he did. And don't go slagging him off.'

'The team turned out last night too, after I called Jimmy Sullivan. He drove her car down here.'

'You've got a good team there, Sean. Look after them.'

'Aye, I know.'

Then they heard coughing as Kara came downstairs. Bracken stood up as she came into the dining room.

'I know what you're going to say: *Why all the racket at this time of the morning?* Was I snoring?'

'First of all, I don't know if you were snoring because I was in my own room,' Bracken answered. 'And secondly, how? Why? When?'

'Sit yourself down. I'm fine. I'll have a raw throat

for a few days and a little cough. Nothing more. The doctor said I was lucky. Another five minutes and I would have been a goner. But I called Bob and he came to get me a couple of hours ago. I can't afford to take time off.' She looked at Chaz. 'We haven't met.'

Chaz stood up and shook Kara's hand just as Bracken's toast popped. He got up to deal with it.

'My name's Chaz Cullen. I work at the city mortuary. I'm a friend of Sean's. And Bob called me to come over for coffee, in case there was any misunderstanding.'

'I'll get you a coffee,' Bob said, coming back into the room.

'How did you know I was up?' asked Kara.

'You sound like a foghorn. No offence.'

'Offence taken.'

She sat down as Bob laughed. He poured her a coffee.

'Any more of that going?' Ed Bracken said, coming into the dining room.

'Aye, sit yourself down, pal,' Bob said, pouring another.

'Well, well, the gang's all here,' Bracken said.

'I had a lie-in this morning,' Ed said.

Bracken looked at his watch. 'A lie-in? No surprise, I suppose. Old codgers are up way before the crack of dawn.'

'Enough of your lip.'

Kara looked at Bracken. 'I never got to thank you properly earlier, so I'm doing it now. Thank you for saving my life. You ran into that fire like it wasn't even there. With complete disregard for your own safety. I'll never forget it.'

'He did the same for me,' Bob said. 'I'll never forget it either.'

'Jesus, you're embarrassing me,' Bracken said, hiding behind his coffee mug.

'Don't be so modest,' Chaz said. 'You're a hero, Sean.'

'Aye, he is that,' Ed said. 'My wee laddie.'

'Not so wee anymore, old man.' Bracken smiled at his dad.

'Sit down, Bob. I'd like us all to have some input here. Sort of brainstorm,' Kara said, and after he'd poured himself a coffee, Bob dragged a chair over and sat at the table, so they were all huddled round it like union conspirators.

Kara looked at each of them in turn. 'Any thoughts on who tried to kill me last night?'

'You thought you saw Tony when you got in there,' Bracken said. 'The fire brigade said it was a dummy, dressed up. It was a decoy to get you further into the room.'

'When I approached, a hooded figure threw in a

petrol bomb. He'd obviously been there for some time, pouring petrol around the room. It looked like the windows and doorway were covered, but not the middle of the room.'

'He wanted you to suffer before you died,' Chaz said. 'Or else he would have spread the petrol around the room more.'

'I hate to say it, Kara, but I think Chaz is right,' Ed said. 'This is definitely personal, and unless your ex has a massive grudge against you, I would look in a different direction.'

'It wasn't him. First of all, he has a new girlfriend. He couldn't care less about me anymore. Plus, I called my old station in Inverness and had them go to his address, after the fire brigade told us it wasn't a human in my living room. He was there with his girlfriend. I didn't have his new phone number, but he still lives in the same flat he moved into after we split up. I have his number now.'

'Somebody down here knows you've moved from Inverness to Edinburgh,' Bracken said. 'How would he find out that information?'

They all looked at him for a moment.

'You're thinking there's a mole in the station. Or one of the team has a grudge, and I can't blame you after what happened a week ago. But I don't know them well enough to be able to tell who would have it in for you.'

'None of your team were told in advance that I was coming. Only Edinburgh's commander knew, and she's unlikely to have tried to kill me.' Silence. 'Don't you think?'

They all agreed that the commander was an unlikely suspect.

'It's somebody here in Edinburgh who knows about you coming back to your house,' Bob said. 'We can try to narrow it down if you can remember everybody who knew.'

'For what my opinion's worth,' Chaz said, 'I would run the names of everybody connected with the move through the system. The moving guys, the estate agents, anybody from the utilities companies. One of them might have a psycho working for them. Then cross-reference their names and where they come from with arson cases.'

They looked at her.

'What? I watch a lot of crime shows.'

'The lassie's right,' Bob said.

'I've already got the ball rolling with that,' said Kara. 'I got Izzie to start the search and she's come up with nothing so far. She'll keep on running the names.'

'I think it's more personal,' Ed said. 'From what you told us about him, he wanted to make sure you were dead. The way he trapped you like that after luring you there. Plus there's not much chance that any workman would know your husband is called Tony, especially since he's not in the picture. This was no stranger psycho. He knows you, and I'm willing to bet you know him.'

'That's a scary thought,' Kara said. 'But I think you're right, Ed.'

'Maybe it's somebody from your past. When you worked here,' Bracken said.

'There is a small connection, but it's not tenuous' she said.

They all looked at her like she was a magician about to perform her final trick of the night.

'Tracey Pitman,' Kara said.

'What about her?' Bracken said.

'You're looking for her because of her connection to Edwin Hawk, in case she decided to murder his girlfriend. She's on the lam right now and nobody can find her. Edwin Hawk was her doctor when she was in the Royal Edinburgh.'

'Hawk told us that,' Bracken said. 'He was responsible for her release.'

'I know. He told me, seven months ago. You see, I was the arresting officer when she burnt down a barn. And Stuart McDonald was the one who made sure she was locked up in the psychiatric hospital.'

'That would make sense,' Bracken replied. 'She's trying to get back at you by burning down the house.'

'It's her MO alright. We just need to try to find her.'

'We'll have a lookout circulated.'

'And see if anybody connected to her drives a short-wheelbase Land Rover,' Bob added.

'Her father's been spoken to, but he hasn't seen her and doesn't want to see her, by all accounts,' said Bracken 'Still, I'll have surveillance keep an eye on his house in case she turns up.'

'Although there's nothing to connect her to the murders so far. It's all speculation,' said Kara.

'There was a piece of newspaper forced down Maxine Campbell's throat,' Bracken said. 'It was dated the second of December, twenty-seventeen. Anything jump out at anybody?'

They shook their heads.

'I can't see what the significance is, but we're trawling the net to see if anything jumps out. It obviously meant something to the killer,' Kara said.

Bracken looked at her for a moment. 'Maybe we're coming at this from the wrong angle. The date on the newspaper was the second of December, but last night was the twenty-seventh. What's the significance of that date?'

Nobody knew. Then something clicked in Kara's head.

'Christ, I should have thought about this. I was thinking about the second and not the twenty-seventh. That was the day Tracey Pitman was put into the Royal Edinburgh. Two days after Christmas. It was a Monday.'

'Here's a question, though,' Ed said. 'When we were playing poker, just you and I having a wee chat, you told me you were going to Glasgow, but at the last minute you were asked if you wanted to come here instead.'

'That's right.' Kara looked at him.

'How would Tracey Pitman know this? How would she even know you were coming back to Edinburgh?'

'I don't know. Maybe she overheard Hawk talking to Stuart McDonald. She was always following Hawk, like a stalker. Stuart asked me along to the Royal Edinburgh to watch as Edwin Hawk assesses Ailsa Connolly. I'll be watching a live video feed.'

'Maybe he let it slip that you're here and are going to watch the assessment. She saw this as her chance to get back at you,' Bracken said.

'That makes a lot of sense.'

'I don't think you should be going about on your own without protection,' Bob said.

Kara looked at Bracken. 'Would you come to the hospital with me later this morning? The assessment is at twelve o'clock.'

'I will. I'm assuming you're not going into the office before you go?'

'No, I think I'll rest up. The doctor said I might feel a bit tired because of the pounding my lungs took.'

'Aye, you go and get some rest, Kara,' said Ed. 'I'll keep my laddie on his toes.'

'Bob, see if you can find my old man some dishes to wash,' said Bracken.

'I have my own dishwasher for that, pal.' Bob lowered his voice. 'She's called Mary.'

Bracken sucked in a breath. 'Dead man walking.'

THIRTY

Bracken was in the incident room when Jimmy Sullivan came in.

'The house is a real mess,' Sullivan said to the team. 'Super Page won't be moving in any time soon.'

'That bad?' Angie Paton said.

'It's a shell,' he said, shrugging his overcoat off and hanging it up.

'It could have been worse, if it weren't for the boss,' Izzie said.

'It was a team effort,' Bracken said.

'You were the only one who ran into the burning building, though. Credit where credit's due.'

'Anyway, how are we getting along on the green Land Rover?' Bracken said, not wanting to dwell on the subject.

Izzie looked at him, turning from her computer.

'There are hundreds of them. Mostly registered to farmers, but a lot registered to other motorists. I'm looking through the names now to narrow the list down.'

'Did Tracey Pitman have a driving license?'

Izzie clicked her keyboard. 'She did drive, but there's no vehicle registered in her name.'

'Keep checking her out – friends, anybody she's come into contact with.'

Bracken looked at his watch. 'I'd better get going. I'm going with Super Page up to the Royal Edinburgh. Jimmy? Keep things going here and call me if you find anything.'

'Will do, boss.'

'Just a quick word before I go.' He led Sullivan out into the corridor. 'I just wanted to say, good job last night.'

'Thanks, sir.'

'But if you've pranged that fucking BMW...'

THIRTY-ONE

Bracken parked in the car park at the new wing of the Royal Edinburgh, where Ailsa Connolly was being housed. His car was sticking out from the space. It pissed him off that whoever had ploughed the snow couldn't lift it over the kerb. They'd shortened the space by a couple of feet. Not life threatening, but it was annoying.

He had called Kara Page and told her he would meet her here, but he didn't see her BMW yet.

He sat in the car and thought about Ailsa Connolly, the woman who had tried to kill him. She was denying it now, of course, and he was now starting to doubt himself. He closed his eyes for a moment, the heat in the car feeling good.

He was sitting that way, listening to the radio, when there was a rapping at his window. He jumped for a second, but then saw Kara Page looking in at him.

He shut the car down and opened the door.

'Sorry to disturb your nap,' she said, smiling at him.

'Resting my eyes for a minute.'

'Sure you were,' she said.

He locked the car and they walked to the entrance.

'You feeling okay?' he said as she started coughing for a moment.

'I haven't had a cigarette all morning. It feels like I've smoked a whole box.'

'Just imagine how your lungs would be feeling if you weren't a smoker.'

They walked in and approached the reception counter, which had glass in front of it. The nippy old sweetie who had been on duty the last time Bracken was here was nowhere to be seen. Then she came into view, but a younger woman approached, one who was smiling. Bracken thought at first that she must be a patient. Surely the staff didn't smile?

'How can I help you folks?' she asked, and Bracken saw she was indeed wearing a staff badge.

'Justice Minister McDonald is expecting us,' Kara said as they showed their warrant cards.

'Oh, of course. He said I was to escort you up personally.'

She buzzed them through and ushered them along

to the lift. Bracken looked in through the entrance to the back office and the old woman looked back at him. He gave her his best fake smile and could have sworn she mouthed *fuck you* to him. But grannies didn't swear. Did they?

Upstairs, the receptionist handed them over to an orderly, who took them through a couple of locked doors until they were in a restricted, high-security area.

Stuart McDonald was waiting, talking with the clinical director, Dr Fritz Meyer. 'Christ, are you okay, Kara?'

'I'm fine. A little raspy, but with the amount of ciggies I smoke, I don't think you'll be able to tell the difference.'

'When we get hold of Tracey Pitman, she'll be rotting the rest of her life away in Carstairs.' Bracken saw Hawk sitting on a chair further along, his head in his hands. McDonald nodded to him. 'Hawk there feels bad, but it's not his fault. That fucking cow fed him a load of pish. I think she was off her nut more than anybody could imagine.'

Suddenly, Hawk stood up. 'Can we get on with this, Stu?'

'Sure, pal.' McDonald turned back to Bracken and Kara. 'You two can go into this room here. We have the live feed all set up. Ailsa's waiting in the other room for Dr Hawk.'

'I'll leave you to this, Stuart,' Meyer said. 'Speak to you soon.'

'Thanks, Fritz.'

The director walked away.

McDonald turned to the American. 'Ready when you are.'

Hawk knocked on the other door and entered, followed by the orderly, who sat on a chair in the corner. McDonald went into the viewing room with the detectives.

THIRTY-TWO

'Isn't Sean coming in?' Ailsa asked, smiling at Hawk.

'Who?' Hawk said, sitting down.

'Don't be coy with me, Doctor.'

'Detective Bracken is in another room. You know how this is going to go. You're under no illusions as to what's going to happen today.'

There were no pads and especially no pencils.

'Good. Then we can begin,' Ailsa said.

Hawk looked at her; she was in her forties but could pass for ten years younger. Married just a week or so ago to a fellow psychologist, a doctor she had worked with years ago; they had rekindled their friendship and then fallen in love. Her husband, Robert Marshall, also worked at the Royal.

'How's your studying coming along?' Hawk asked.

'Extremely well.'

'Church of Scotland minister, isn't it?'

'Yes.'

'That's quite a different approach from what you were used to doing. I attend a small church in my hometown. We have a fantastic pastor who really knows his stuff.'

'Have you suffered a loss recently?' she asked.

'What?'

'Did you lose somebody close to you?' There was no smile on her face but a look of sympathy.

'Why would you ask that?'

'Your eyes are red, Dr Hawk. Unless the drink has taken hold of you – in which case I doubt Justice McDonald would have let you conduct this interview – then you appear to have been crying. Too early in the season for allergies.'

Don't get personally involved. That was his remit, but Stella was smiling in his mind right now, and he could hear her laughter if he tried hard enough.

'I've read the reports on how you've been doing whilst in here,' he said, ignoring her question.

'Was she somebody special?' Ailsa asked.

Hawk made eye contact with her. 'I'd like to ask you about your feelings towards the men you killed.'

'Girlfriend? Is that it? Men rarely cry over a breakup, so I'm guessing you lost her in the sense that she passed on.'

He probed a tooth with his tongue, thinking that maybe he shouldn't be here, but now he was, his very reputation was on the line.

'How's your husband doing?' he asked.

'Robert's fine. We see each other every day. We have lunch together. But you knew that. You know everything there is to know about me. How I killed the men who had gone unpunished. Men who were evil to their core.'

'Is that how you feel about men now? Is that how you're seeing me?'

She gave a wry smile. '"It is better to light one small candle than to curse the darkness,"' she said.

'Eleanor Roosevelt,' Hawk replied.

'Indeed. I am no longer in the darkness, Dr Hawk.' She gave him a matronly smile. 'Tell me about her.'

He took a couple of deep breaths before answering. 'I loved her, but somebody took her away from me. We had our lives planned out, but the light at the end of the tunnel was snuffed out.'

He was screaming in his head to stop, but he was losing it. He had to keep on the right track.

'She must have been special. I know you didn't have anybody when you started working here. You were here just before I arrived from Carstairs. My husband worked here as well then.'

'I know Robert well.'

'He's a big fan. He's always liked your books. He has them all. He's a compulsive book buyer. He won't get through them all, but he likes to see them on his bookcase. And that Kindle he has, well, let's just say Amazon made it too easy for him to buy more books. At least the ebooks don't take up much room.'

'I often talked to your husband about books. Robert is a very well-read man.'

'So was Stella.'

He was speechless for a moment but kept eye contact. She hadn't said it in a threatening way, but he had to carefully form his next words to her. Saying *How did you know?* would have tilted the power in her favour.

'She was an avid reader. That's how we met.'

'I know. Robert told me she would ask him all about you, as you would spend time in the canteen talking about books.'

Hawk nodded, then composed himself before carrying on.

THIRTY-THREE

Bracken watched the verbal sparring going on between Ailsa and Hawk.

'She's giving him a run for his money,' Kara said.

'She's treating him with kid gloves,' Bracken said. 'She has one of the best minds. I know.'

McDonald looked at him. 'Do you think she's really changed, or is she playing it up for the camera, as it were?'

Bracken looked at the screen, looked at the woman who had killed six men like it was nothing.

'I think she's a different woman from the one she was back then.'

'What's to stop her killing somebody again?' Kara asked.

'What's to stop any of us killing? In the right circumstances, would you kill for a loved one? When you thought it was Tony tied to that chair last night, would you have killed the perpetrator if he was going to kill Tony before your eyes? Would you have killed him if he was a threat to your life, which he clearly was?'

Kara didn't answer.

Then Bracken's phone rang.

'Excuse me,' he said. He stepped out of the room, into the corridor, and walked away from the two rooms.

'Cameron, how's it going?'

'Fine, boss,' Cameron Robb said. 'Are you sitting down?'

'I was sitting down. I got up to answer the phone.'

'You're going to love this one. We got the dental records from Stella's ex-husband. Well, we got the name of her dentist anyway. We got the records and took them to the mortuary where the post-mortem was taking place, and the pathologist compared the X-rays with the corpse. And wouldn't you know it, the woman who was burned on that old college campus in Kirkcaldy wasn't Stella Graham.'

'Are you sure?'

'It was double-checked by the high heid yin himself. Whoever she was, she wasn't Stella Graham.'

'Jesus. Are you still at the mortuary?'

'I am.'

'I'm going to hang up. I need to talk to somebody and then I'll call you back, pal.'

'I'm not going anywhere. I'll be right here.'

Bracken cut the call and went back into the room. 'The body we found on the old college campus wasn't Stella Graham,' he said to Kara. 'Dental records don't match.'

McDonald turned to him. 'Who is it?'

'That's where I need your help, sir.'

'Anything.'

'Make a phone call for me.'

'Sure. Where to?'

'Here. I need you to call the hospital's clinical director.'

'I can do that. What do you want me to ask him?'

Bracken told him what he needed.

McDonald stepped out and returned a few minutes later.

'He's on it right now. It won't take long.'

'There won't be a problem with cutting through the red tape, will there?' Kara asked.

'Not at all. I still have some power in this city,' McDonald said.

They watched the proceedings with Ailsa and Hawk. Then a few moments later, an orderly stepped in with a file.

Bracken thanked him and took the X-rays out of

the file and took photos of them, both upper and lower jaw. Then he sent them in a message to Cameron Robb.

His old DI sent a message back. *Doc is going to check right away. Hang fire.*

Bracken could see Kara's leg bouncing up and down like she needed to pee. He wondered if he should join in and start biting his nails but held back.

Minutes went by, and for a moment Bracken thought the wall clock was knackered, the second hand was going so slowly.

Then his phone rang and he answered it, not bothering to leave the room this time.

'You were right, sir. The corpse is Tracey Pitman.'

THIRTY-FOUR

'What do we do now?' McDonald said.

'We wait until Hawk's finished with Ailsa,' said Bracken. 'We owe her that much. Her life is basically on the line now.'

'I'm going out to the corridor. I'll call Jimmy Sullivan,' Kara said.

'They probably have smoke alarms in the toilets,' Bracken told her.

'Crap. I'll still call him anyway. Give them a heads-up.'

She left the room and Bracken looked at the screen again.

'Tell me, sir, what do you think the chances are of Ailsa getting out of here?'

'Ninety-nine per cent. As long as she doesn't fuck this up and rip his balls off. But she's made remarkable progress, and if I thought for one moment that she wasn't capable of becoming a normal member of society again, I wouldn't be doing this. Why? What do you think? What's your opinion?'

'I think that last week she could have killed one of us, but she didn't. She sees life in a new light now, and what happened is behind her. I think she has a rock in Robert.'

'Good. I was starting to doubt it when I saw her asking Hawk about Stella.'

'We have to find out where the hell Stella really is. And why somebody would want us to think that she was dead. And who would want to kill Tracey Pitman.'

McDonald nodded to the screen. 'It's not him. He can thank God I was with him when Stella went missing or else I'd be instructing you to get a warrant for his arrest.' He blew out a breath. 'If not him, then who?'

'The same person who killed Maxine Campbell.'

'Different MO.'

'They have a connection. All three women do – Maxine, Stella and Tracey. They were all here in the hospital at the same time. Maxine was a social worker, Stella a psychiatric nurse and Tracey a patient. They all interacted.'

'The only other connection is Hawk.'

'You said he was with you,' Bracken said. 'It's somebody else who has a connection and we need to find that connection. If he went to the trouble of making us think that Stella was dead, then he has an agenda. But only he knows what that is.'

Bracken stared at the screen. Stared at Hawk. He was looking at the key right there.

THIRTY-FIVE

Hawk was sweating when he finished.

'That concludes our interview,' he said.

Ailsa smiled. 'I see it as a wee chat, Dr Hawk. Getting to know one another a little better.'

'All we needed was a cup of tea and some of those little sandwiches you British prefer, with the crusts cut off.'

'Alas, I'm not a bread person. Scones and jam, now that I could go for.'

They stood up and the orderly did likewise.

'Nice meeting you, Dr Hawk. Stay safe.'

He was about to turn away, but he stopped and looked at her. 'Is that a threat?'

'Do you consider it a threat?'

'It can be perceived as one.'

'The threat is not from me, but whoever killed

Stella. He did that to send you a message. You're not safe, Dr Hawk. A man who can burn a woman to death like that is not stable.'

'How did you know how she died?'

'We get TV in here. And newspapers. The dead woman was found in Kirkcaldy. Stella came from Kirkcaldy. She told me that herself when we spoke. And yes, I've spoken to her on many occasions. She told me all about you.'

'Why would my life be in danger?'

'Did you think that he would stop after killing Maxine? She and I were friends, as much as any social worker can be friends with an inmate. Again, she spoke very highly of you, just like everybody else who talks about you. But you must have had a cast-iron alibi, or else they would have been looking at you as their main suspect. You probably were until you provided proof, so it stands to reason that there's somebody else out there killing people. If it was just random, I wouldn't say you were in danger, but you're the one person who's in the middle of the triangle. Two workers and a patient. One of those workers you had a personal relationship with. I may be way off base here, but it doesn't feel like it.'

She smiled at him again. 'Good day, Doctor.'

She was escorted out of the room and taken through another door before Hawk came out.

Bracken and McDonald were waiting for him.

'Give me the edited version, Doc. Do you think she could be trusted to be released?'

Hawk was still thinking about her when he looked at the justice minister. 'I would release her under supervision at first, for a couple of months, so she can adjust to life outside, then into the total care of her husband.'

'I must admit, I had doubts,' McDonald said. 'When she started talking about Stella.'

'I wouldn't have recommended release if she hadn't. If she'd agreed with everything I said and hadn't acted like that, I'd have thought she was putting on a show. But I saw the real Ailsa in there.'

McDonald smiled and nodded to Bracken. 'Go on, tell him.'

'Tell me what?' Hawk said.

'The body we found in the burned-out college building in Kirkcaldy wasn't Stella.'

'What? What are you saying?'

'The dental records didn't match. Long story short, she's been identified as Tracey Pitman. Somebody wants us to believe Stella is dead.'

'And she isn't.'

Bracken held up a hand. 'All I can say is, that's not her in the mortuary in Kirkcaldy. Let's not get our hopes up. She has to be somewhere. Somebody took her. Killed Tracey and put Stella's driving licence down Tracey's throat to stall us.'

'Why would he do that?'

'He has an end game. And I think you're a pawn in all of this.'

THIRTY-SIX

The incident room was buzzing when Bracken got back to the station with Kara.

'There's no mistake?' Jimmy Sullivan asked as Bracken took his overcoat off.

'None at all. Two pathologists confirmed the dental records matched the teeth in the burned corpse. Tracey Pitman.'

'Why would he put Stella's licence in Tracey's throat?' Izzie asked.

'It's a stalling tactic. He wanted to throw us off the trail until he's ready to play out whatever game he's playing,' Bracken answered.

He walked over to the whiteboard and looked at the names and photos on there for anything that might jump out at him.

'We have Stella getting the train over to Fife, and

when she gets to the station, she goes to her car. What happens then?' He turned to the team.

'She's intercepted by our killer,' Sullivan said.

'Yes. But there were no phone calls from the public about somebody struggling. He got her into another vehicle, leaving hers behind. He was taking a risk. There might have been another passenger coming off at the same stop. Even if there was nobody else there, he wouldn't take that risk. He's very methodical. He had this planned out down to the last detail. He did some research and found the abandoned college campus just along the road from the station. He was confident when he took Stella. Not only that, but he already had Tracey.'

Bracken looked at them each in turn. 'They knew him. That's why they went willingly.'

'Why would Stella go with him when her own car was right there?' Angie Paton asked.

'He's very persuasive. I think he let the air out of one of her tyres so she would immediately jump into his car. He told her something that would make her panic,' Bracken said.

'We know she was divorced from her husband, but her abductor must have said something to get her into his car. Whatever it was, it worked. He took her and somehow they ended up at the college,' Sullivan said.

'We can assume that Tracey was already there,'

Angie said. 'The train got into the station at nine-ish, and the fire was reported at ten-thirty, give or take. We know that he'd poured petrol inside, so if he'd lit the fire at nine then the call to the fire brigade would have been at around that time. The place would have gone up in minutes. He must have taken Stella along to the college. It's in the same direction as her house and if she saw he was heading in that direction, she wouldn't be suspicious. By getting her into the car, he'd have had control of the situation. She trusted him so getting into his car wasn't a problem.'

'What excuse would he make to her to get her into the car?' Izzie asked.

'It would have to be something realistic. Something believable right away, something she wouldn't question,' Kara said.

'We know it wasn't Tom, her ex-husband. He was in the pub. It had to be somebody she trusted, somebody she knew well enough to take him at his word.'

'Do you think that Tom would have arranged a friend of his to pick her up?' Angie asked.

'I think she would have been wary of this,' Bracken said. 'Why would she trust any of her ex's friends?'

'I still think he could have told her something was wrong with Tom. They were married at one time, and even though you're divorced, sometimes you still care about the person you were married to. Like me and Tony,' Kara said.

Bracken stared at her. 'You're right. He knows them well enough to be able to tell them something happened to a loved one, or an ex. He knows you, and he knows Stella. I'm willing to bet he knew all about Maxine Campbell, our first victim. The one thing that ties you all together is Tracey Pitman. The question is, if he'd already killed her, why try to kill you? It seems that he thinks you all did something to him. If we find that out, we'll find our killer.'

THIRTY-SEVEN

'I'm just going for a wee walk,' Ed Bracken said to Mary.

'Alright, love. St. Margaret's Park is just down the road. It's a nice area to walk in. Any of the side streets off the main drag will take you down to it.'

'Actually, I'm going to trawl the charity shops. See if I can pick up some books.'

'There are plenty of them round here. I'm sure they'll have something for you. What sort of books do you read?'

'Westerns. I used to read crime novels, but listening to my son going on about real-life crimes kicked that into touch for me. It's a wonder I'm not reading romance novels just to keep my head straight.'

Mary laughed. 'Well, if you do see some romance

books you fancy, pass them to me when you're finished.'

They both laughed.

'Sean said he'll help me out with my bill at the end of the week, and he said he wants to pay the going rate. Make sure you take it, hen. This is a smashing wee business you have going here, but it doesn't run itself.'

'Well, I don't know...'

'Well nothing. You have bills to pay and this is a luxury guest house. Keep the prices high, keep the riffraff out. Sean can afford it. I'll make sure he pays his way.'

'We feel funny charging the full price, especially since Sean saved Bob's life.'

'As my old mother used to say, there's no sentiment in business. If it wasn't for you, Sean would be reading his books by candlelight in some manky old hovel. You'll be getting the full rate, just wait and see.'

'You can stay as long as you like, Ed Bracken.'

'Alas, my Max will be tearing my pal's house apart; he'll be missing me. So the first of January, I have to go home.'

'Well, come back any time. We always have a wee room we keep a bed in for emergencies. We have nieces and nephews down south who come up for a visit sometimes, and if we're fully booked, they bunk in there. You're welcome to bunk there, and bring Max with you. We love dogs. Bob would have one in a heartbeat, but we're too busy running this place to have one. A visiting dog would be good, though. He's housetrained, isn't he?'

Ed laughed. 'Oh aye, he is that. If I could only teach him how to make my bed in the morning, I'd be laughing.'

'If I could teach Bob to make the bed, I'd be laughing too.'

Ed went outside into the cold air, careful not to slip on the pavement, which was still slick. The last thing he needed was to fall and break a hip. Mickey couldn't look after Max for the long term.

He was standing at the bottom of the driveway, about to walk towards the main shopping area, when a car with blue flashing lights behind its front grille pulled into the side of the road and the passenger window was rolled down.

'Ed Bracken?' asked the man behind the wheel.

'Who's asking?' Ed said.

The man held out a warrant card. 'DI Cameron Robb. I was sent here to look for you. Get in. I need to take you to Sean.'

Ed opened the passenger door and got into the car. 'What's happened, son?'

Robb held up a finger. 'Hold on.'

He put the siren on and carefully did a U-turn,

then headed back along the Glasgow Road. He weaved in and out of the traffic, going through the red light at the foot of Clermiston Road.

'What's going on, son?' Ed asked again, feeling his heart racing. It would have been the same if somebody had told him Max was ill, but his son was a close second.

'I have some bad news, Ed. Sean was attacked by somebody while he was searching for the killer he's been hunting. He's in a bad way, and they wanted me to take you to the Royal in Dunfermline. I'm going to get us there as quickly as possible.'

'Oh my God.' Ed took his phone out.

'You can't call him. He's in surgery. I'm sorry, Ed, but it looks bad.'

'Jesus.' Ed opened up the photos app and started looking at photos of his son. 'My God. I hope he pulls through.'

He looked down at the photos and started crying. Then, while Robb was trying to navigate the Drumbrae Roundabout, Ed switched apps.

By the time Robb nearly had them in front of a bus, the photos were back and Ed's phone was on silent.

THIRTY-EIGHT

Sean Bracken took his phone out of his pocket. 'Hello, Dad. What's up?'

No reply, but he could hear noises in the background.

'Christ, have you arse-dialled me again? What have I told you? I'm busy here, so if you've lost your meds again, ask Mary or Bob for help. If you've lost your marbles, I'll be taking that bloody phone off you.'

Just the ambient noises on the other end, and Bracken was about to hang up when he heard his father speak.

'You're a good boy, Cameron Robb. Coming all this way to pick me up. I hope my son doesn't die before we get there.'

'What are you talking about?'

'I'll have to call my daughter. Sean would want his sister there.'

'No!' the other voice answered. 'I won't have time to pick her up as well. It's just you, Ed.'

'I have to tell her, son. She doesn't know where the Royal in Dunfermline is.'

'I said no, Ed. Sorry. But no can do.'

Bracken felt ice running through his veins as he heard the siren in the background. He knew this was all wrong. He didn't have a sister. He turned to Izzie and Kara, covering the phone.

'Somebody's got my dad. Somebody pretending to be Cameron Robb. I heard him talking and it's not Cameron. Somehow, he got my dad into a police car. I can hear the siren. He said they're going to the Royal in Dunfermline. Have the locals wait there. Jimmy, find out what kind of car Cameron was driving; see if they have GPS on it.'

'Will do.'

'Izzie, try to track my dad's phone.'

'Are you sure, Sean?' Kara asked.

'Yes. My dad mentioned my sister. I don't have a sister. And something about how he hopes I won't die. The killer's done the same as he did to Stella. Got my dad in a car. Now I need you to think. This is beyond Stella and Maxine and Tracey now. He tried to kill you, but why would he take my dad?' he asked Kara.

'When we arrested Tracey, she was living in Fife.'

'Why would you be arresting her in Fife when you worked here?'

'I was working in Fife at the time. Before I came here. Cameron and I were the arresting officers.'

'Christ, he's trying to get us all. If he's killed Cameron and taken his car, then he's going to try to lure me somewhere with my dad, just like he tried to lure you by saying Tony was at your house. Where the hell would he be taking him?'

'I have no idea.'

Bracken listened to the phone again. His dad must have switched the sound off, so if Bracken was talking, the man masquerading as Robb wouldn't hear, but the line was open and Bracken would hear his dad talking.

He could only hear the sound of the car engine revving now.

Izzie was trying to trace the number Bracken had given her when Angie Paton spun round in her office chair. 'I kept on going through the list of civilians who have a small green Land Rover. And one name came up.' She pointed to it on the screen.

'Christ.' Then Bracken heard a voice talking to him and it wasn't Ed.

'You listen to me, Bracken. You want to see this old bastard alive again, you come and get him. Bring that bitch Kara Page. Only her. You hear me? You know

where to come. If you haven't figured it out yet, then you'd better get a move on.'

'Hey, less of the old,' Bracken heard his dad say, then he heard skin on skin as if Ed had just been slapped.

'If my dad's dead by the time I get there, you're next.'

Clearly, the killer had the phone now, because he heard Bracken. '*Big words.*'

The connection cut off, and when Bracken tried calling Ed again, there was no sound.

He called Edwin Hawk's number. It went to voicemail. Bracken felt like leaving a message telling him what he would do to him if he harmed his dad.

'Look at this,' Sullivan said, pointing to his computer screen. 'The last known address for Tracey Pitman isn't where we thought it was. We have a patrol car waiting near that house in Dunfermline, but that's not what's on here.'

Bracken turned to Kara. 'Where did you arrest her?'

'It was a farm property north of Dunfermline. There were three fires in barns around that area. She was caught after the third one.'

'Check this out,' Angie said. 'I just did a search for arson fires in Fife and those three came up. Then I cross-referenced fires in that area with the date on the bit of newspaper that was put down Maxine's throat. Bingo. A house was set on fire northwest of Dunfermline on the second of December twenty-seventeen. A woman and teenage girl died in the fire.'

Bracken looked at the screen for a moment. 'That's it; he's going back to the scene of the crime.'

'We can have the locals on scene in a matter of minutes,' Kara said.

'No. He's not there yet. If he's approaching and he sees the marked cars, he could kill my dad. He wants me to go there. With you.'

'Whatever it is he thinks we did, he's got Cameron, and now he wants me. You're involved in this because you're leading the investigation,' she said to Bracken.

'We need people here to man the phones and computers.'

Kara turned towards Jimmy. 'Stay here and help them.'

'I'm coming too,' said Sullivan. 'He won't see me when we get there. I'm not letting you walk into a trap.'

'Alright,' Bracken said. 'Grab a coat. And when we get there, don't let anybody belt you over the heid with a log of wood.'

'You're never going to let that go, are you?'

THIRTY-NINE

'Bastard,' Ed Bracken said. 'Who belts an old man in the face?' He tried to staunch the flow of blood.

'That's for trying to get one over on me. Old fuck. Now get out, and if you try to make a run for it, I'll break one of your legs.'

Ed got out and looked around him, at the old, burnt-out house and the surrounding fields. 'Where am I supposed to run to? There's snow everywhere; it's freezing cold. What is this place anyway?'

'Home sweet home,' the man said as he looked up at the house, half of which had been burnt out. The extension tacked on to the side had fared better, and if only they had been in there, they might have been safe. But the petrol poured around the house had made sure they were trapped.

'Get inside. Turn to the left. If you try any funny business, you'll get what's coming to you.'

'Haven't you forgotten something?' Ed asked, nodding to the back seat of the car. At the object that had aroused his suspicions in the first place.

'Don't need it anymore. It was merely a prop.'

They walked into the house. It was almost a relief as they stepped inside, out of the bitter wind.

Ed turned left. He wasn't sure if this man had a weapon or not, but it wasn't as if he could fight him.

The man took Ed's phone out and turned it back on. He called Bracken's number and listened as the detective answered.

'You have half an hour. If I see any other police cars, then your dad dies. I will stick a knife in his carotid. He'll bleed to death before anybody gets near. If you don't make it in time, then he'll die. It's in your hands now, Bracken.'

FORTY

Snow was coming down again as they passed through the west part of Dunfermline and headed back out. There were farms along this road with high hedges.

Bracken pulled into the side of the road. 'You've got five seconds!' he shouted. Sullivan was out of the car in three.

Bracken shot off, then slowed the car down further up the road before turning into the driveway that led up to the old house.

'Mother Nature's taking over again,' Kara said as overgrown bushes and trees slapped at the car. The driveway was covered in snow, but they could see a car had been up here recently. There were no cars parked outside the front door of the house.

Or what was left of the house.

Then they saw the old, white van parked on the other side of the house.

'No sign of Cameron's car,' Kara said.

'Or the green Land Rover. Maybe they're hidden in a barn or something.'

The front door of the house was gone and so was part of the roof. A tarpaulin had been put on at one time, but it had done little good. Debris from inside the house that had been thrown out by firemen lay scattered on the front lawn, or what was left of it, and was being covered with snow.

They could smell the petrol as they walked to the doorway.

'You could stay out here. You've already been in a burning house,' Bracken said.

'So have you,' Kara replied, gently pushing him in.

They smelled a mixture of mould and petrol as they moved further into the house. The left-hand side of the building was mostly intact, so they went in there.

'This smells like my house last night,' Kara said, looking around at the charred walls.

They checked the rooms and saw nothing. The floorboards were old and weak and moved underfoot as if they were about to give way at any moment. Then they went to the back, and that's where they found Edwin Hawk and Stella Graham.

Each was tied to a chair, with a lit candle balanced

on a plate on their head. The candles had been burning down steadily so that there wasn't much left to them.

Both Hawk and Stella were staring at Bracken and Kara.

'Jesus, Sean. Thank God you're here,' Hawk said. 'He's a lunatic. You have to get us out of here.'

'Where's my dad? And Cameron Robb?'

'He took them out of here. He said me and Stella were the main targets. Everybody else was collateral damage.'

Bracken could see Hawk's candle wobbling. 'Stop talking.'

Bracken's phone rang. He saw it was a FaceTime call. He answered it.

'Hello, Sean. I see you got there in time. Well done.'

Donald Masterson was smiling at him on his phone screen.

'Where's my dad?'

'He's safe. For now. Say hello, Sean's dad.' Masterson flipped the picture and Bracken could see his dad sitting on a couch holding a cotton hanky to his nose. It had blood on it, but it was the object in Ed's other hand that caught his attention.

'He's an old man. Why don't you let him go?'

'I will. But I want you to listen to me first. Those two in front of you; I want them punished.'

'What did they do?' Kara asked.

'Tracey Pitman was arrested for setting fire to three barns. She was put into the psychiatric hospital, where she underwent treatment for three years. Then the great American Hawk there decided she was no longer a threat to anybody, and released her. She was in love with him. That doesn't bother me. What does bother me is the fact that at one of his book signings I overheard him telling Stella that he'd released Tracey and then Tracey had confessed that she'd set fire to the very house you're standing in. My house! My wife and daughter died. It was deemed an accident. The power had gone out that night and my wife was using a kerosene lamp, so they said, and she must have dropped it and started the fire. But Tracey admitted she was in my house and set it on fire.'

'Hawk couldn't have known that before he assessed her for release.' Bracken looked away for a second, his eyes catching Sullivan quietly coming into the house. Hawk saw him, but Sullivan put a finger to his lips. He very carefully watched every step until he reached the pair tied to the chairs, then he blew the candles out.

'He knew after she told him! And it wasn't just Hawk who was responsible for her release; Maxine Graham and Stella were responsible too! He asked for their opinion, and they gave it to him, which swayed his decision. So I killed Tracey. I had you looking for her, thinking that Stella was dead. I used her to draw Hawk to the house.'

'What about Maxine?'

'She died too soon. She came back to the Writers' Museum and walked in on me with my arm around Tracey's neck. She'd forgotten the signed book. We were all away, and they left me at the bus stop. I walked back unseen by them. Maxine wasn't at the same bus stop, so I didn't know she hadn't got on a bus. Tracey was just slipping under when Maxine saw me, and then she screamed and tried to run out. I grabbed a scarf from the coat rack and put it around Maxine's neck, but she was still struggling. I tried to stab her with a pencil, but she put a hand up. That angered me, so I fought harder and she eventually succumbed. I carried her out like she was drunk and sat her on the bench. I was going to put her into one of those large bins, but she was too heavy.'

'Were you going to burn her?'

'Of course; I was going to set fire to her house. But at least she was dead. Some social worker she was, letting Tracey go.'

'Now I've heard your story, I'll make sure that Hawk and Stella are punished for what they did,' Bracken said.

'Good.'

'Why did you burn Kara's house? She was just part

of the arresting team when they caught Tracey. She had nothing to do with her release.'

The picture flipped back round to face Masterson. 'What are you talking about? I never burned her house. Why would I waste my time on her?'

'Her house had petrol poured in it and set on fire.'

'Don't try and land something on me, Bracken. If I'd burnt it, I would tell you.'

Bracken tried to keep the surprise out of his face. 'Let my dad go.'

'No can do. I'll keep hold of him until I hear about what will happen to those two, then I'll let him go.'

'You mean that, Donald? I mean, I can trust you, can't I?'

'Of course he does, stupid boy!' Ed shouted. 'Scout's honour!'

'There you go, Sean; Scout's honour.'

Masterson cut the FaceTime video and Bracken put his phone away. He heard somebody come in behind him and turned round, thinking it was the curator himself, but it was Cameron Robb.

'Jesus, sorry, boss. He called me saying he was some chief superintendent from Edinburgh and he wanted to speak to me. When I got here, he smacked me over the head with something.'

'He walks with a walking stick. Maybe it was that.'

'He knocked me unconscious, and when I came to,

I was in the back of that van outside. Jimmy there untied me.'

Bracken looked at Hawk. 'We saw you have a green Land Rover registered to you. Where is it?'

'I sold it before I moved to America,' Hawk said.

'Who to?'

Hawk paused for a second. 'Maxine Campbell.'

Stella looked at Hawk. 'She hated it. She thought it would be a fun vehicle, but she got rid of it. She didn't tell you because she didn't want to hurt your feelings.'

'Who did she sell it to?' Bracken asked. 'Because it's still registered to him.'

'I don't know,' Stella replied. 'She drove it once before she got it insured and hated it. She never drove it again.'

'I need to go and get my dad.'

Jimmy was untying Hawk and Stella. 'Do you think he'll let your dad go?'

'Of course not.'

'It seems strange he would just let us go,' Stella said, standing up.

'Don't knock it. The guy's a crazy asshole,' Hawk said. Then he saw the look on Stella's face.

'What's wrong?' Bracken said. He followed Stella's gaze down just as the first tendrils of smoke rose through the floorboards. Then there was an almighty whoosh as the cellar caught fire.

'Run!' he shouted, grabbing Kara by the arm to stop her stumbling. They made it outside just as the first of the flames exploded through the floors and started to consume what was left of the house.

Kara was coughing uncontrollably and Bracken held on to her as she bent double. She leaned against him as she straightened up.

'You okay, boss?' Sullivan said.

'I'll be fine.'

'I'm sorry about that bastard getting my car,' Robb said to Bracken.

'That's okay, son. I'm going to get it back for you.' Bracken turned to Kara. 'Ma'am, call this in. Hawk, you look after them. The boys and I are going to get my dad back.'

'How do you know where he is?' Hawk asked.

'Because he told me.'

FORTY-ONE

It would have been like a drive in the country if Bracken wasn't giving the impression he was suicidal.

He had been quiet for the journey, which had only taken ten minutes so far.

'Are you going to tell us where we're going, boss?' Sullivan said.

'That idiot showed me my dad sitting on a couch. It was my dad's own couch. He was holding a toy that belongs to his German shepherd, Max. And he gave me another clue: *Scout's honour.*'

'What does that mean?' Sullivan asked.

'The Scouts' Scotland Headquarters are in the grounds of Fordell Castle. There's also a mobile home park there. It's where my dad lives,' Bracken said as he raced along Aberdour Road, crossing over the M90. He only had the blue flashers on and he switched them off as he got onto the B road. 'Just round the corner. We'll have to go in as if we're just visitors.'

Bracken turned to the right and was surprised to see the road had been ploughed well. He stopped the car in a parking space outside one of the mobile homes.

'Jimmy, we're going to have to go through the neighbour's gardens. My dad's house is the fourth one down on the right.'

Robb opened the door and got out, keeping low. He didn't shut the car door all the way. Sullivan did the same, and Bracken cut the engine before getting out.

'Slow and steady, or shock and awe?' Robb said.

'How about you two go through the side gardens, and on this side you'll see a bathroom window. It's got frosted glass and the catch is broken. The window will swing in. The windows in the living room face the front and the other side. The kitchen windows face this way, but hopefully he's not looking out the kitchen window. I'm going to go to the front door and ring the bell. Maybe he'll come and see who it is. If it's my dad, then I'll wing it.'

The two men nodded and set off running, keeping low as they leaped the first small fence. Bracken jogged down to his dad's mobile home and didn't hesitate but walked up to his door and rang the bell.

He looked over to see Robb and Sullivan leap the small fence into his dad's garden. He looked up the side path and saw Robb climb through the bathroom window while Sullivan went round the back.

Donald Masterson answered the door and stepped back. This door led into the kitchen.

'I've been waiting on you, Sean. Come in.'

'I thought you might be, Donald.'

'Take it nice and easy and your dad won't get hurt.' Masterson stepped back and then Bracken could smell it again. He was getting used to the smell of petrol thrown about a house.

'It's over. Your house went up like a tinderbox, especially with all the petrol you'd poured in the cellar. I was the only one who got out. Hawk and Stella were still tied to the chairs. They're dead.'

'I knew you would kick that wire! I told myself, that clumsy clot with his big feet will catch that fishing line. It went down through a hole in the floor and was attached to a box of lit candles. Crude but effective.'

'You've got what you wanted, Donald. I've come to take my dad back.'

'Not quite. You're a part of this, whether you like it or not. You're the lead investigating officer. You're not going to just walk away and forget this happened.'

Bracken said nothing but slowly walked towards Masterson, making him walk back into the living room.

'That's far enough, Sean.' Masterson brought a

lighter out and flipped the top, lighting it. 'Ed! Get out here.'

Nothing.

'Ed. Stop playing games! Get out here! Sean's here and he wants a word.'

Nothing.

Bracken saw the man was starting to get annoyed. Then he looked back, out through the kitchen window. Robb, Sullivan and Ed were climbing over the neighbour's fence, although Ed wouldn't win any Olympic medals for jumping a hurdle. If there was a gold medal for clumsily half-throwing yourself over and landing on your arse, then it would be his.

Bracken watched as the two detectives grabbed an arm each and then they were gone from sight.

Masterson stepped backwards and looked down the little hallway and saw the sliding doors at the end were open.

'Bastard!' he screamed and threw the lighter down.

Bracken turned and ran, just before the flames caught hold. He stopped for a second and saw Masterson engulfed in flames, screaming and flailing. Then he was out of the door and running up the road as the flames ate his dad's house.

He was out of breath by the time he got to the car.

'Dad!' he said when he saw Ed standing with the two other detectives.

'Glad you got my message with Max's toy,' Ed said, smiling. 'Maybe you could help me clean the place up. That maniac poured some petrol on the floor.'

'Yeah, about that...' Bracken looked at the thick black smoke rising into the air.

FORTY-TWO

'You decided to come to the party with me after all,' Chaz said to Bracken. 'I feel honoured.'

'You should be. I had plenty of other offers, but I felt sorry for you, so I decided to come along with you.'

'Yeah, that's it. Norrie Nae Mates had a ton of invites.'

He laughed as she drove over Ravelston Dykes. 'I really did get an invite, but I thought I'd rather come to your party.'

'I'm glad. It's been a hell of a week.'

'It has that. Both Kara and Ed have nowhere else to go, so they'll be staying at the guest house for the foreseeable future. And my dad will be getting his dog back tomorrow. Max will be coming to live at the guest house too. I just hope the old man is prepared to get up in the middle of the night with him.'

'I'm sure it will all work out in the end.' She looked at him. 'You know you can always come across to my place for a bit of relief.'

'Just a coffee and watching some TV would do.'

'Christ, Bracken, you know I meant relief from the crowd. There you go again; I'm the hoor of Corstorphine.'

He smiled at her.

'Did you believe Masterson when he said he didn't burn Kara's house?'

'I'm not sure. He had nothing to gain by lying, but then that begs the question; if it wasn't him, then who was it? And why?'

'That's two questions.'

She crossed over Queensferry Road and down Craigleith, and parked down from the townhouses.

She stopped her car and smiled at him. 'Angie told me she'd invited you along here tonight too. Imagine the beamer you'd have pulled if you'd knocked me back and then I turned up here.'

'Beamer? Like the one you have right now?'

'That's all you.'

She laughed as they went into the townhouse. Kara was there, as was Dr Pamela Green and other members of the team. Not Jimmy Sullivan, though; he was home with his wife and kids.

They had a good time, had a few drinks, Chaz

sticking to soft drinks. Then midnight crept up on them.

'Happy New Year,' Chaz said. Bracken kissed her under the mistletoe, then his phone rang. He thought it would be his daughter, but it was Cameron Robb.

'Happy New Year, Cameron, son. You're a bit keen, if I do say so myself.'

'Happy New Year, boss. But I'm calling because I got a call from one of the CID team who are on call. He was bored, so he was playing around on the computer. And guess what he dug up?'

'Don't keep me in suspense.'

'Mark Turner, your daughter's potential new boyfriend?'

'What about him?'

'His father's Billy Turner. The bank robber. The man —'

'I shot dead,' Bracken said, finishing his sentence. 'I need to go, Cameron. Good job, son.'

He hung up and called Sarah.

'Hi, Dad. Happy New Year.'

'Listen, honey, is your boyfriend with you?'

He could hear music playing loudly in the background, then the sound of her leaving the room and moving somewhere quieter.

'Say again?' she said.

'Is your boyfriend there? Mark.'

'Nah. He dumped me a couple of days ago. He said we weren't right for each other. I think it's because you're a copper, but if he's that insincere, then stuff him.'

'Okay. Be careful.'

'I will. Love you, Dad.'

'Love you too.'

'Fancy a dance?' said Cheryl. Angie's wife. He smiled at her and had a dance and they had fun, but Bracken's thoughts weren't far away from Mark Turner. Maybe it was all a coincidence.

He didn't believe in coincidences.

Half an hour later, he caught up with Chaz. 'I'm going to head off now. I said to my dad I'd have a wee dram with him before morning. But you can stay and have more fun.'

'You can't get rid of me that easily, Sean Bracken.'

'I don't want to be a killjoy.'

'Let's just say our goodbyes and we can go and have a drink at the guest house.'

'Are you sure?'

She hesitated for a moment. 'I'd feel safer knowing I'm with you.'

'Let's go.'

'Thank you again for everything,' Kara said. 'See you at breakfast.'

'Yes, ma'am.'

They drove back to the guest house. Chaz stopped the car and looked at Bracken. 'I know you said this is going to pass, and I know it will, but I'm not going out on my own anymore. Not for a long time.'

'You got Scrabble in the house?' he said.

'And Monopoly.'

They got to the door and Bracken opened it and was met by a ferocious furball with a mouthful of teeth.

'Max! Down!' Ed shouted, coming to the door. 'See who's here,' he said to Bracken.

'I see him.'

Chaz looked like she'd peed herself; then the dog came up to her, wagging his tail.

'Mickey brought him over earlier. Max loves Bob and Mary already.'

'One big, happy family,' Bracken said as the German shepherd put his head between his legs and rubbed. 'One big, happy family.'

AFTERWORD

Thank you for reading this, the second Sean Bracken novel. He will return in book three, titled, Crossing Over.

I would like to thank the gang for their input. You make a great team! A special thanks to Ruth, from Police Scotland. And to my wife and daughters, who make it all worthwhile.

Anybody who knows me knows I love German Shepherds. I've had four. Max was my first, Bear is my latest, and I couldn't help myself, putting yet another one in my books.

Thank you to you, the reader for climbing aboard this train with me. If I could please ask you to leave a rating or a review on Amazon or Goodreads, that would be fantastic. It only takes a few minutes and greatly helps a writer like me.

AFTERWORD

Until next time, take care my friends.

John Carson
New York
February 2021

Printed in Great Britain
by Amazon